Jonathan's Leap

To all my friends in the dance world,

who are the best!

Jonathan's Leap

Celia Purcell

HULTON BOOKS

Published by HULTON BOOKS
First published 2014

1 3 5 7 9 10 8 6 4 2

A CIP catalogue record for this book is available
from the British Library

ISBN 978-0-9927497-0-5

Printed in Poland

Hulton Books
4 Torbay Road, London, NW6 7DY
www.authoizationuk.com

Chapter One

Jonathan stood in the middle of the front row. He wore a white T-shirt and black tights, and with his feet prised in fifth position, he felt like Nureyev. This was his favourite hour. After school on a Monday and a Thursday, Jonathan came to the Neptune Arts Centre for ballet with Miss Spencer. He was twelve years old and the only boy amongst girls who whispered together in groups and never noticed that he could jump higher than a frog.

'Stick your bottom in,' hissed Mia from behind him. She was fully made up for a disco and had high-kicking legs, but she didn't have Jonathan's elevation. He had told his mother that Mia's *jetes* went only five centimetres off the floor and when she landed, everyone shook from the vibration. Jonathan knew his opinion didn't count for much. Mia had a great future, they said. His own intention when he was old enough was to go far beyond the chorus line. He wanted to stand centre stage and hold a cygnet with lots of white tutu net round her bum.

Two boys from another school were training at White Lodge with the Royal Ballet and he knew of three at the next town's Viewpoint Academy who had got into *Billy Elliot* the previous year. Jonathan had a long way to travel.

'May I have your curtsies, please, girls,' said Miss Spencer. She was pencil thin, her hair scraped back viciously with an elastic band. 'And a nice bow from our male contingent . . .'

The pianist played some chords from Fauré. Jonathan bent towards the mirror and tried to get his nose down to his knees.

'Very good, Jonathan,' Miss Spencer said.

She wore black and her feet barely skimmed the surface of the floor as she came forward.

'At least you look as if you've finished a performance,' she said.

Two of the girls started to giggle and nudge each other.

Jonathan was filled with a sense of mission. 'I have,' he said.

* * *

In the front hall after class, Jonathan practised his bow again, facing a torn poster for job recruitment. The children waited to be picked up, chattering loudly as visitors came in and out of the building. Some were reluctant to be there. They only took ballet because their parents thought that the exercise was good for them. Others had total commitment and arrived early.

The Neptune often put on shows during the holidays such as *Griselda and the Magic Mice* and *Visions of Batman*. These involved a lot of sleepless nights for the mums who were bullied into making costumes. Some mums just didn't have it.

Playing Batman had not, in Jonathan's mind, improved his career prospects. Wearing his dad's 60s 'shimmy shimmy shake' jacket in the nightclub scene was the most embarrassing thing that had ever happened to him. Every extra tassel his mum put on for the occasion had fallen off and then his trousers had split. Jonathan hadn't spoken to either of his parents for three whole days after that.

Mia was usually the star. She played Griselda, of course, all pout and frolic, which wasn't how Griselda was meant to behave. That was what Jonathan thought, anyway. But her mum was very good with a sewing machine. She made delicate chiffon skirts and waistcoats that were fit for performers. Mia was a pain when she played the lead, but she was beautiful. She had glossy hair and eyes that shone ambitiously under long, fluttery lashes.

Now dressed in boots and a denim jacket, Mia took on the demeanour of a shrew. She stood chewing gum and staring at Jonathan.

'Stop showing off,' she said. 'You do nothing but prance about.' Mia blew a bubble and let it spatter onto her cheeks.

'Get lost,' said Jonathan.

He went on practising because he knew that it infuriated Mia, and also because he liked it. Anyway, his mother would be the last parent to arrive. She always was.

When she came, her entrance reminded Jonathan of a whirlwind out of control.

'Sorry, darling! I've had a rush to get here and the traffic was awful.' Charmian Morrison kissed her son lightly on the head and, still on the move, she grabbed his hand.

'Don't do that, Mum,' hissed Jonathan.

She was always in a hurry these days no matter where they were or what they were doing. Sometimes he wanted to ask her why she rushed around, but he never did. His mother was no good at keeping schedules, which was part of the trouble. And she wasn't really a 'ballet' mum. She tried very hard to be, but every time she sewed buttons onto brocade or made a witch's hat it came apart.

Mrs Morrison had taken a full-time job recently at a garden centre that involved display work and advising customers. Since her first day, she had more or less stopped cooking at home. Jonathan and his father were sick of pizza and salads. So far, they had remained staunchly carnivorous. Their burger take-aways were usually munched together in secret.

Jonathan found himself thinking of food at this very moment. 'Have you got any cakes, Mum?' he asked in the car.

He was packaged between some carrier bags and an ancient typewriter.

'Help yourself,' Mrs Morrison said.

She was having trouble with the ignition and getting more stressed every time she turned the key. Jonathan took a chocolate brownie from a packet in one of the bags. They were on the eighth floor of a shopping mall car park and the view was getting cloudy.

'Mum, there's smoke all round us,' said Jonathan.

Someone was knocking on the front passenger window.

'Your exhaust has dropped off,' a male voice shouted.

His presence was nowhere to be seen and he remained invisible, a genie who might later make a more mystical pronouncement.

'Thank you,' Mrs Morrison called back.

Her hands were very white and when her eyes caught Jonathan's in the mirror, he saw that they were filled with tears.

It was autumn. The journey home was in slow motion. Jonathan watched the way streets glittered under artificial light and how pedestrians walked briskly towards the Tube. If these people were the ones who went to work, Jonathan pondered, then they all looked the same. None of them saw further than a pavement slab ahead, all in their dark, shapeless clothes. He was suddenly glad that his dad wasn't among them because he would be lost in the crowd. A nobody. He wouldn't be any good at being a nobody. Mum said that the trouble with Dad was that he was far too busy thinking he was somebody. She had told him so only last night.

Jonathan liked spending time with his dad. Often they escaped together to the shed at the end of the garden that smelt of oily rags and tools. Mr Morrison would light the wood-burning stove while Jonathan watched its flickerings take shape on the wall in front of him. There was the horse with the long neck and a series of birds that flew above dusty shelves.

Sometimes his father banged away with a hammer. They had moved to the suburbs from town four years ago but he liked to think of the shed as his 'rural retreat'. In the corner, he kept his spade and a few bags of smelly compost for what was a garden without real layout. It was just a sloping terrace that led down to an acre of grass, a line of trees and the guinea pig hutch.

Mrs Morrison didn't mind Jonathan dancing. Jonathan hated sports, so she felt the exercise out of school was important. Now she was beginning to realise how serious he was, but her husband took no interest. Mrs Morrison thought his attitude was due to depression.

'I don't want my son prancing the boards. It might become a habit,' he had told his wife when the classes took off in earnest.

'Suppose he's good,' she replied. 'Miss Spencer says Jonathan's got real stage presence and that we must give him the chance. Lots of boys are performing these days. Some of them earn real money too.'

Mr Morrison peered for moments at the ceiling. He

tried not to relive an old memory.

'It's a rotten life and hardly a profession for normal kids,' he said at last.

Mrs Morrison had put her hands down flat on the kitchen table at this. 'Jonathan is a perfectly normal boy but he has an abnormal father,' she said, staring through the window into the garden.

Mr Morrison stared out too, but he didn't know what he was staring at.

'The exhaust dropped off,' Jonathan said as soon as he and his mother got home. 'We spluttered all the way.'

His father was on the computer in his study. His eyes kept to the screen.

'For God's sake, Charmian,' he said, 'didn't you take the car in for its service last week when I was away?'

Mrs Morrison was busy with the shopping and Jonathan didn't wait for her answer. Home life was too predictable. He ran out into the garden and tapped Barnaby's cage. The guinea pig was his very own and only a year old. Nothing happened at first. Then a bristle of whiskers appeared through a pile of straw and newspapers and Jonathan saw his nose quivering.

'Hello, Barnaby,' he said.

The animal came nearer until Jonathan could feel his skin tickling.

There was a keen wind. The garden moved restlessly, as though in the grip of unknown forces. Jonathan opened the hutch and took Barnaby close to him so that he nestled into his collarbone. It was a position they were both accustomed to. The sky was black and forbidding. Jonathan looked up towards where he thought Heaven must be.

'Oh God,' he whispered, 'please find Dad some work very soon ...'

He wanted to go on but there were other wishes crowding in and Jonathan knew he shouldn't think about them now. For a long moment, he stood with Barnaby, very upright and still, until the warmth of the guinea pig made him happy.

Chapter Two

Jonathan first saw the notice one morning in half-term. He was strolling behind his mother at the time and whistling casually, which was what he often did when forced to be seen out with her. As they passed the town hall, Jonathan caught sight of some words on a plain white poster stuck to the advertising board.

Dancers wanted, aged 10 to 13, for a production of Sinbad The Sailor *playing at the Albany Theatre, December through January. No previous experience necessary, but some ballet technique vital, as is enthusiasm and commitment. Audition at The Cellars, 10 a.m. Saturday November 9th. Rehearsals begin November 25th.*

'Mum!' Jonathan had shot high into the air. He was trembling with excitement. 'Look!' he shouted.

Mrs Morrison's schedule today was already giving her a headache. She had been on the phone for two hours earlier, contacting suppliers for more tulip bulbs. They were selling fast. Three of them were due to call her back and she had yet to buy school shoes for Jonathan, whose feet had reached ridiculous proportions.

She peered short-sightedly at the advert above Jonathan's head. Mrs Morrison smiled despite her worries. 'Oh, Lord,' she said. 'What on earth will your father have to say?'

Jonathan was racing up and down as if he were unable to stop. 'I've got to go, Mum,' he panted. Coming to a halt, he flung his arms out to embrace the world. The gesture was as good as an athlete's victory wave. This time Mrs Morrison laughed. She couldn't fight Jonathan's enthusiasm. But his obsession for performing was certainly not from her side of the family.

Her mobile phone vibrated in her bag. 'Just a second, Jonathan,' she said.

Charmian Morrison couldn't waltz without stepping on her partner's toes. Before her marriage to Peter, their first serious date had taken place to a background of soul numbers. She had made him giggle at her lack of co-ordination. Charmian was willing to learn and she would follow her future husband very out of step as he strutted across the disco floor with his fingers clicking.

Even she had to admit that he had good hip action and Charmian didn't mind making a fool of herself. She was also pretty, and when she laughed at his jokes, which she did frequently, her blonde hair rolled back in a thick torrent from her shoulders. Charmian's untidiness was another attraction, and made Peter want to protect her. Often she would have a button missing or her skirt lopsided like an overgrown schoolgirl.

Now that he had lost his job, he felt obsolete in more ways than just employment. In the beginning, Peter scoured the media pages and went through countless application forms. To compensate, Charmian had filled her life with activity. The management were often phoning for his wife from the garden centre now . . . people that Peter didn't know and who referred to him – slightingly, he thought – as 'Mrs Morrison's husband'.

Advertising had been his world and he had moved successfully through a career in the fast lane from copywriting to eventual creative director. But from there, his position had soured as every day became a political minefield to negotiate. In April, he and the MD had differed in opinion over a major client's branding and not long after that Peter had been made redundant. He had stopped applying to companies now because they never replied.

He was not far off fifty, that was the problem, and it didn't help to see Charmian immersed in a world of her own making, which seemed to exclude him.

Lately Peter had taken up oil painting in his shed, having bought a very expensive book on art. Van Gogh was a favourite. Peter fancied himself as a post-Impressionist. Under solar lighting, he had completed one canvas of a bunch of tulips on a blue-check tablecloth. Jonathan had helped to arrange the composition. Over the last few weeks, Peter had been struggling with a bowl of fruit, a wooden figure of a deer and a cauliflower. Several cauliflowers and assorted fruits had long since gone into the recycling bin.

Charmian was only forty-three and had begun to find her husband's lack of drive irritating. He didn't seem to live for the present. The other day she had found him in the loft going over old family photographs that showed him as a spotty adolescent under the dour gaze of his father. Peter's mother had died when he was young and he never spoke about her.

Next to shots of Morrison Senior rambling the hills above their farm was a picture in sepia tones that Charmian had never seen before. A ballerina with a wasted and tragic expression stared out at her from *pointe* position, arms raised in what seemed to be a halo over her head. She wore tulle that wafted about her slender legs, too perfect to be real.

'Who's that?' Charmian asked.

She had entered quietly and peered now over his shoulders.

Peter slammed the album shut as he turned towards her. 'Stop creeping up on me!' he shouted. A red blush blotted his forehead as it did without fail when he was angry.

Charmian suddenly felt herself grow cold. 'I'm not,' she said, and for a moment Peter was someone quite foreign to her.

Now she sighed. Jonathan was gripping her arm.

'You will let me try out, Mum, won't you?' he pleaded and his eyes were large saucers that shone brown and implacable, just like his father's.

'What about school?' Charmian asked. That was another problem. Jonathan and his education. He just wasn't interested.

'I'll fit it in, Mum, honestly I will,' he said.

There were geese flying overhead and as they keeled to the left, they made loud, honking noises which filled the air. Jonathan followed their graceful arc until they disappeared from sight and there was nothing left in the sky but the blur of clouds heavy with rain. He wanted to fly too, far away from here and take off with the sort of leap that would remind people once again of Nureyev.

The following week at the Neptune Arts Centre, everyone was talking about *Sinbad The Sailor*. Mia had insider knowledge because, as she told the class, her mum knew the rehearsal director whose name was Bill Jones.

'He doesn't want any podgies, either,' she said in the passage outside the girls' changing room.

Manoeuvring her left hand under her left instep, she carried her leg into a side *developpe*. Then, slowly pivoting on her remaining foot, she went full circle until she came face to face with Jonathan.

'That means you,' she said to him, and her accompanying smile wasn't sweet.

Jonathan decided to ignore Mia. He had work to do.

The buzz of conversation continued even as *pliés* started. Despite a line of pupils along the *barre* with heels in first position, none of them were ready. From the CD player came the delicate sounds of a Chopin sonata. The three-four rhythm was as instilled in Miss Spencer's head as a clock ticking, but there was little sign of her children hearing it. Enough was enough.

'Stop, everyone, at once!' she cried and clapped her hands for silence. Miss Spencer pressed her finger on the *pause* button and drew her mouth into a thin line of disapproval. She was losing weight and she knew it. Her grey tunic skirt was held together with a safety pin and she was only too aware these days of her shallow chest under her crossover cardigan. A long time ago, she had made her soloist's debut as the nubile Juliet – slim as a reed but with body curves in all the right places.

'Listen to the music,' Miss Spencer said. 'You cannot be true dancers without hearing your accompaniment.'

She released her finger again, allowing Chopin back into the room. It was where he belonged.

As Jonathan bent down with his knees turned out as far as they could go, his back ached and he felt a click in his right hip. He came to the upright position too fast.

At the end of the sequence, he inclined his head as Miss Spencer had taught him, aware that most of the girls were still moving. They put Jonathan off. No wonder he couldn't concentrate.

When they came to preparation for *pirouettes*, the entire class seemed to totter and several kids fell over. Only Mia could manage a full turn and stay on balance. She closed in fifth and nodded by divine right.

'Good, Mia,' said Miss Spencer.

Jonathan had given up and was standing in the corner. He decided to strike a pose anyway and made to cross his arms haughtily, looking up into the far distance as though he might see someone arriving by chariot.

'None of you are using your spot,' Miss Spencer said. 'It's no good turning unless you train your eyes to a spot on the wall.'

Jonathan felt very dizzy. 'I'm seeing a lot of them already,' he replied.

Mia and a couple of the older girls laughed. They were always laughing.

'You're not doing it properly, silly boy,' Mia simpered.

Miss Spencer was used to these interruptions. 'That's enough for today,' she said and avoided looking at Jonathan because sympathy right now would be inappropriate.

As the children began to leave, Mia did a last turn to establish herself.

'Wowee . . .' she said.

Jonathan had caught her hair in his face as it sprang away from a tightly coiled bun. The colour reminded him of sacred flames.

Despite the warmth of her office at the end of class, Miss Spencer shivered while she changed into her street clothes amongst the paraphernalia of junior gym equipment. She drew her heavy winter coat close to her. She was so cold. Yet there were beads of sweat on her forehead.

Miss Spencer bent double as the pain hit her somewhere in the region of her abdomen. It was becoming familiar. She gave a groan and fell against the wall for support. A minute passed. Then Miss Spencer breathed more easily. She did up the buttons of her coat with methodical fingers.

The class was coming on . . . She might have some of her own pupils to coach during the *Sinbad* run. Mia stood out, but Jonathan was a raw talent. Despite his bulging stomach, the boy had a tremendous leap. She hadn't seen anything like it for years. Who could tell? What a stroke of luck that Bill Jones had been able to find her after so long. Now she had the chance to come back as ballet mistress for a proper production. Miss Spencer knew that the next few weeks were very important, and she was going to have to stay as healthy as she could.

Chapter Three

There were red crosses all the way down Jonathan's exercise book. They flared off the pages like a series of SOS signals until the last two sums – which were slashed across entirely. Underneath in capital letters was written *SEE ME!*

The maths teacher stared into a distance far beyond Jonathan. She had been a fixture at the school for many years and was not sympathetic to those pupils who could do better. Right now, Mrs Humphries felt her adenoids twitching. She took out her handkerchief.

They were alone together in the classroom that had been abandoned minutes before. Broken chalk lay on the table between them and a jumble of figures loomed incomprehensibly from the blackboard.

'The trouble is, Jonathan . . .'

Mrs Humphries was coughing again. She heaved with great gasps from the bottom of her chest and, for a few seconds, turned puce. Her eyes watered and she blew her nose until the noise stuck in her throat.

'. . . I haven't got a stream low enough for you to go into,' she said finally.

Jonathan was using this moment to flex his pectoral muscles, which took all his concentration. But he nodded anyway.

Mrs Humphries tapped her pen across a series of multiplication tables. 'How can nineteen times sixty-four possibly come to two hundred and forty?' she asked.

There was silence, broken by children racing past the windows.

'I don't know,' Jonathan said at last.

'I'm going to have to speak to your parents about private tuition. You don't even understand the basics.'

Mrs Humphries had begun to wave her handkerchief in a vain attempt to contain a sneeze. Jonathan thought she might cry. He relaxed his pectorals.

'Can I get you a glass of water, Mrs Humphries?' he asked.

She was rocking in her chair and continuing to wave

helplessly. 'Off you go,' she said between coughs and Jonathan left the room.

Afterwards he wondered whether Mrs Humphries would live until the next maths class.

In the playing fields, a rugger game was in progress. Several boys were veering to the left as the ball moved incessantly out of reach. Trails of mud surrounded them and when they dived into a scrum, they took the form of some giant and cumbersome crab. Jonathan couldn't see his best friend, Alex. He was probably at the bottom of the pack. He usually was.

'Pass!' yelled a voice and then another.

The referee blew his whistle. Jonathan shivered. Every time he gave verbal support, a fog clouded his vision and the trees that lined the pitch seemed gaunt and unwelcoming. There were only a few spectators there, trudging amongst piles of leaves to keep warm.

Alex was running now unchecked, zigzagging his way towards the upright posts. As he came parallel, another boy fell in beside him and dived for his ankles. But it was too late. Alex had got the ball past the post. Lying on the ground, he waved his arms aloft in triumph.

'Hugs Bugs says I've got to have private lessons,' Jonathan said when he and Alex were trudging back to the changing rooms along with the other players.

'Hard luck,' said Alex. He wasn't much good at maths either but he was better than Jonathan.

It was November fifth and school was over for the day. The lights were out in the top floor classrooms and most of the kids had left for home.

'You've got mud all over your nose,' Jonathan said to Alex.

'So what?' replied Alex. 'Just because you don't like games.'

Jonathan gave his friend a shove. 'Dancers can't do games. They use different muscles.'

Alex wiped his face with the sleeve of his rugger shirt. 'I told my dad about your ballet lessons and he said he was glad you weren't his son.'

Jonathan didn't wait for anything more. He aimed a punch at Alex's middle, hitting him hard. Then Alex hit him back.

'Steady on, you guys!' shouted the referee. He was right behind them.

'Your dad doesn't know anything,' said Jonathan.

They walked on together, just thinking.

'Too right,' said Alex, 'though I guess he was talking more about the expenses.'

Jonathan dug his toes into the path, where cement had taken on the glitter of approaching frost. The night would be cold.

He knew he had to slim down. When he stood sideways to the mirror in his practice clothes, Jonathan could see the beginnings of his father's beer gut. But if he pulled his stomach in, his ribcage stuck out. Jonathan didn't like his legs either. They were short and stocky. Not like any of the guys in *Billy Elliot*, or TV dance competitions for that matter. But he had a cool, floppy fringe and when he went up in the air, he liked the way it fell across his forehead as he came down again. His face wasn't bad either, with a normal smile despite the loss of an upper tooth. But what was really missing were cheekbones. Jonathan wanted cheekbones, the type that Nureyev displayed in every photograph.

Above Jonathan's bed, Nureyev looked out from an old colour poster in the guise of Count Albrecht. He wore a brocaded tunic, a wide sash and some very smart boots. They were brown and so shiny, somebody must have recently cleaned them. Nureyev was smiling because he had just completed a series of *jetes en tournant*. Fancy doing leaps in a pair of boots! Jonathan had learnt some of the steps by heart. He also knew that Giselle was just out of shot and that the story didn't have a happy ending. His mum was going to take him to see the Royal Ballet production soon and he would be able to tell her all about it. She had promised.

As for *Sinbad*, Jonathan had no idea who he was except that he must be an Arab if the story was from *The Arabian Nights*. That was what Mia had told him. Perhaps the producers would want foreign-looking dancers, but then they would have said so on the poster.

His mum warned him not to tell Dad.

'Let's see how you get on first,' she said. 'After all, we don't want to get him worked up for nothing.'

Jonathan frowned. 'Why doesn't he like me dancing?' he asked.

His mother took a long time to answer. 'He doesn't think it's a proper job for grown ups.'

The old Peter had been so easy going, Mrs Morrison thought sadly. A year ago, he wouldn't even have minded about the maths.

Several of Jonathan's friends were coming over to the house for a fireworks display. Already, there were shooting lights in the sky and explosions that whistled and sang overhead. Barnaby had been taken inside to the safety of a cardboard box and Peter was now busy erecting a rocket launcher against the trellis in the garden. Afterwards, he began a bonfire with newspaper and charcoal.

When the children arrived, Mrs Morrison wished they hadn't.

The doorbell rang again with short, sharp bursts that sounded urgent.

'Damn!' she said.

Kayla and Amy were both from the Y ballet class. Kayla had spots and chewed gum incessantly. Jonathan said it was because she was unhappy about being taller than all the other girls. Amy was born to be a mouse. Whenever she was asked a question, she would shrug, put her hands in her pockets and look vacantly ahead as if everyone around her were mad.

There were four boys from school, including Alex. Jason was a big, tall guy and nobody messed with him. And could he run! Jonathan had seen him on the field. Sam and Marcus were both good at figures. In fact, Sam was a whiz kid and not only was he Hugs Bugs's favourite, but he spent a lot of time in the holidays flying between England and the US. His parents were fighting for custody and his mother lived in New York.

Mr Morrison put a match to the first firework. Nobody

spoke, and there was that moment of anticipation before it fizzled out. The second and third matches broke.

'Here,' said Jason. He tossed a box over to Jonathan's father. He was cool.

The rocket, on reaching the sky, was red, white and blue.

'That's the American flag colours!' yelled Sam. He was kicking the base of a tree hard in his excitement.

'Don't do that,' Mr Morrison said. 'The tree has a life too.'

Jason slapped Sam around the ears. 'Dead right, Mr Morrison,' he agreed.

Mrs Morrison was jumping up and down to keep her circulation going. Her husband lit a Catherine wheel without success. The girls started to jump too, and then they began to play a hopping game.

'What's happening, Dad?' asked Jonathan. He was balanced carefully on one leg.

'Come on, darling,' said Mrs Morrison.

They were all feeling the cold.

Alex came rushing out on to the patio. 'I think your kitchen's on fire!' he shouted.

Mrs Morrison screamed. She began to run towards the house. 'Help,' she cried, her voice almost lost in the wind. 'I forgot the sausages . . .'

Mr Morrison remembered Jason now. He was the boy who had been sick over their sofa two summers ago.

The oven was belching smoke but there were no flames, just an air that drifted grey and thick over every surface and made them gasp. Everyone stared at the tray of sausages turned to coal sticks.

'Wowee,' said Jason. 'That's brilliant, Mrs Morrison.'

At nine p.m. Mr Morrison went to lie down. He felt his pulse, which was rapid even though he had tuned into the radio and Schumann's Dichterliebe. A fine tenor voice sang German songs of love on a summer day.

Mr Morrison let his gaze wander over the bedroom and noted the fading paintwork. A top shelf was lopsided and needed replacing while, directly above, there were ominous cracks in the wall. He patted the space on the bed where his wife ought to be. The flatness of the mattress worried him, as if he was destined to be alone. He had to get a job.

Next year, Mr Morrison thought to himself, there might not be any fireworks at all.

Chapter Four

They were nearly late for the audition. The car wouldn't start and when Mrs Morrison finally got the engine running, there was rain. Jonathan had his rucksack ready. He was nervous and annoyed.

'Come on, Mum,' he said from his seat next to her, willing her into action.

The car bumped noisily over an adjoining road and past a straggly village. Rain slid in sheets across the windows but only one windscreen wiper was working. The other was bent and dragging a piece of foam that flopped about uselessly.

When they met the motorway to join the rush hour line of traffic, Jonathan pinched his mother's wrist.

'Don't do that, darling,' she said, but she wasn't concentrating.

Monotonous fields passed them by. All the cows were lying down. On reaching the town, Mrs Morrison was forced to pull up at a pedestrian crossing. An old lady had appeared almost under the bonnet. She was bent double and her painful walk with a stick was the longest Jonathan had ever experienced. When she arrived at the other side, she faltered and began to turn round again.

'You had better get out and help her,' Mrs Morrison said. 'She seems to have lost her way.'

Jonathan pursed his lips. He was about to argue.

'Off you go,' said his mother.

Jonathan stepped out of the car and took the old lady's arm. A cold air seeped into his lungs as he found himself taking most of her weight. Jonathan was glad he was so strong. From the safety of the pavement, the lady fumbled for her purse and took out a coin.

'Thank you,' she said. 'You're a good lad.' When she smiled at him, her gums were pink and toothless.

As the car picked up speed again, Jonathan looked at the coin in his hand.

'It's a Euro,' he announced. 'You and Dad can use it on holiday.'

Mrs Morrison kept her gaze ahead. 'That won't be this year, and not the next probably,' she said carefully. 'Anyway, what about you?'

Jonathan didn't answer. He wasn't going anywhere with either of his parents until they stopped arguing. He had more important matters on his mind. Jonathan was developing a sore throat and was thankful that he wouldn't have to sing.

The Cellars was a dump. Formerly a nightclub, the place had been turned into a community centre with rehearsal rooms at the back. There were puddles of water around the entrance and a couple of drunks sat huddled for warmth by the door with a bottle of cider between them.

'Better hurry up,' said one of them, who was tied up in the bottom half of a sleeping bag. He wore woollen gloves that his fingers peeped through. 'They're all there and waiting for you.'

Jonathan couldn't swallow. He took out his practice clothes in a tiny room where three other boys were already changed and stretching. They seemed to know each other. As Mrs Morrison unravelled his tights, a terrible thought came to him.

'Mum,' he whispered, 'those boys are from the Parkview

Vocational Trust. They train in the Russian method.'

Jonathan wanted to go home. He knew he didn't have a chance pitted against the talents of Parkview pupils. They were the ones who had their own audition for the Royal Ballet School – and who mostly got in.

Mrs Morrison was staring at Jonathan's tights as he put them on. 'I'm afraid there's a small hole at the back,' she said, 'and I've forgotten to bring a needle and thread.'

His mother was lying. The hole wasn't small. It started at the centre seam and had grown into a ladder that went across his left buttock.

'Two minutes!' shouted a woman from the doorway. 'And could you come straight to the basement rehearsal room.'

The boys were excited and flexing their feet. One of them was facing Jonathan. He had wonderful arches, but that wasn't all. As Jonathan met the boy's gaze, he saw a fringe thicker than his own and, below it, the sort of cheekbones that made ridges.

'I can't go in,' Jonathan said desperately.

'Nonsense,' said Mrs Morrison.

She had worries about this professional-looking bunch too, but she pushed Jonathan until he was forced to join the children making for the stairs.

They were all waiting now and blocked off from the main room. There was a smell of cleaning fluid and a dampness that seemed to emanate from the very floorboards themselves. Some kids had adults with them who were not helpful. Everyone was shoving and making too much noise. Mrs Morrison counted twenty-eight heads and then gave up because the heads kept on moving.

Someone was prodding Jonathan in the back. 'You've got a big hole in your tights,' said a female voice.

It was Mia. She stood in a pose that was distinctly non-balletic, her legs planted across the corridor. Her hair had been plaited and shone through a dozen bun grips. Mia's mother was also there, carrying her daughter's woollen wrap.

'Not to worry, Jonathan,' she said. 'I'll have that sewn up in a jiffy.'

She was already rummaging in her bag and then they were getting left behind as the wave of applicants surged forward.

'It's all right, Mrs Nathan,' Jonathan said and he wouldn't have cared now if the whole audition had been called off.

He wanted to pee too. Instead, Mia's mother had

taken a handful of his tights and was subjecting him to yet another humiliation. The two mothers chatted as Mrs Nathan expertly wove her needle in and out of the fabric while Jonathan was forced to bend forward. Mrs Nathan was dance mad and always cheerful. She lived for the day when Mia would reach stardom.

'What a jam,' Mrs Morrison said, and as she spoke the basement door swung open and the children, without a backward glance, almost fell into the room.

'Good luck, darling,' she called and she gave a sigh of relief. Jonathan's tights were intact.

'Thanks a lot,' she said to Mrs Nathan, who was anxiously watching her own daughter's posterior.

'I think Mia's frill is crooked,' she muttered. But it was too late to do anything more.

Jonathan hadn't even had a chance to say goodbye. There were so many people around him, he was edged against the corner of the *barre* on one side and an upright piano on the other, where a man sat hunched over a dozen scores. They were being ordered into the centre of the studio and told to sit.

Nobody spoke. A skylight in the roof had gone grey with the rain and Jonathan could hear drips landing at intervals into some unseen bucket at the back. Condensation seeped through the walls.

A man was talking now.

'I'm Bill Jones,' the man said, 'and I'm here as director of *Sinbad*.'

He glanced at the many faces fronting him without humour. He was of medium height, wore his hair in a ponytail and a gold chain around his neck. Bill's eyes were chilly, though Jonathan was glad to see that he had a weight problem too. It was surprising how lightly he moved on his feet, and when he used his hands to express something, his whole being came alive.

A girl with a notebook sat next to the director, her expression bored, as if she had been through this process many times before.

'All right,' said Bill.

He was in his mid-thirties and this morning felt his age. He had promised himself and Reg that there would be no more pantomimes after this season. No more draughty rehearsal rooms and actors with prostate trouble.

He had had enough of children too. Earplugs helped but they were no good when some child was screaming into his lugholes. A quieter life was what he and Reg were intending. They were booked for cruise work next March.

Bill strode through the crowd of children, dividing them expertly into four groups. Jonathan was in group D.

'Ten minutes to warm up and then, when I call your group, be ready to start.'

Jonathan moved against one of the *barres* but he couldn't find enough space to allow freedom for his limbs. He tried to point his toe to the front and then to the back. It was useless. Even worse, he was sideways on, which meant his stomach and his bottom stuck out.

Jonathan caught sight of the same boy from their changing room. No problems for him at all. The boy had found himself a space up ahead and was at this very moment practising an *arabesque*. Sure enough, his back was beautifully arched, like a Russian dancer, and his leg lifted high into the air. Jonathan knew that the competition was going to be tough.

Mia had made herself available. She stood in the front line of group A and while Bill gave his instructions, she fiddled with her pink leotard frill and rose up and down on her toes. The others weren't so lucky. Both Kayla and Amy were in the second group, and hunched as closely together as people on the Tube.

Jonathan didn't have to see Amy to know that she would be nervously twiddling her thumbs. Next to her, Kayla's head loomed high above the rest like a wary giraffe. She didn't look too good. Come to think of it, nobody did.

Group A was being called by the girl with the notebook. Bill was deep in conversation with the pianist and when he came away, he was muttering.

'I want skips,' he said, 'just simple skips round the room . . . The mood is happy, as if you are out to play. Greet your friends. Now let's have a large circle, please.'

There was chatter while the children found places. The pianist was sweating. He was small and seemed overwhelmed by the heavy coat that fell out in folds over the floor around him.

When the music started, the skips were heavy and behind the music. Bill tapped the piano top with his knuckles.

'Enough!' he called.

There were one or two notes missing that sounded vital to Jonathan. He did a little jig at the side while he waited.

'Can you keep still?' one of the Parkview boys said to

him. 'I've got to concentrate.' He had a shaved head and a tattoo on his left arm.

The kids were jumping again and then they were galloping. Mia's steps were more like a sedate canter and she took longer than anyone else to get into the air. That was typical of her . . . She was just getting started and she only had eyes for Bill.

Jonathan recognised the next tune. 'On a Wonderful Day like Today' came across from the keys with special emphasis on the third beat. He was perking up. By the time Group D had come on, the song was playing for the umpteenth repeat.

'Stop!' yelled Bill. He plucked at his gold chain and twisted it until his skin went white. Then he clicked his fingers. 'Faster, Reg,' he said. 'They're sagging.'

Reg got his second wind and began another number. They were into step full changes and small leaps, but Jonathan couldn't find his stride. His elevation for the day was not working. In fact, the whole thing was too fast now and the boys from Parkview were jumping much higher than he was.

As he began his last series of jumps, Jonathan's shoe elastic broke. It was the catastrophe he had always dreaded. This was his most important hour and his equipment was falling apart. There was nothing else to be done. He would have to retire and forget all about *Sinbad*. Jonathan stood back and tried to look as if everything was normal. He knew right then that he was finished.

Chapter Five

'*Take it off,* you moron!'

Jonathan was dully aware of Mia. She had obviously come to gloat over him.

'Take your shoes off,' she said. 'You can dance without them.' She was stooping down and lifting his right foot up as if he were a horse.

'Shhh . . .' said Jonathan. He wanted to hit her and he wanted to cry at the same time.

'Next!' called Bill.

He was beginning to separate the children, noticeably favouring the ones given to cheesy smiles. During a break, the girl assistant wrote their names and addresses in her pad. The lucky ones fidgeted with excitement and assessed remaining candidates as if they had every right. Bill and Reg were talking again. They were obviously friends.

Suddenly Reg banged the piano lid down and stood up. 'I've heard that song before!' he said bitterly to Bill and he closed his music score deliberately.

Jonathan held his breath. Nobody spoke. The two men communicated now in low voices that couldn't be heard, even though the children had gone quiet.

When the door opened, it was a welcome interruption. A small bird-like woman entered the room and, as she did, a shaft of sun came down from the roof window and lit up her space. Although smothered in scarves, Jonathan knew who she was straight away. Very precisely, the woman unbuttoned her coat.

'Miss Spencer!' Bill came close to embrace the woman. She was half his size. 'It's wonderful to see you,' he said. He kissed her on both cheeks.

Mia's expression was incredulous. 'They know each other,' she whispered. Her hands were on her hips and she was craving to see more.

Jonathan felt something close to elation. But would she recognise him on a day when his talent had so deserted him?

Bill came forward again. 'Right, boys and girls,' he

said, 'let's see what you can do. This is your last call and I want you to give it everything you've got.'

He was sizzling with energy now and working out a combination of steps one after the other. Jonathan felt the back of his head, which was wet. Miss Spencer would realise that he was suffering from nerves. He had learnt that most dancers had the same problem. She was alert now towards the children. They were following Bill as he taught them the 'farmer's step' in a series of box patterns, four by four.

When the moment came to dance, Jonathan was very aware of his bare feet, and also that he was on the wrong leg. He seemed to be hopping sideways too when everyone else was going forwards.

'Who's the short plump boy?' Bill asked Miss Spencer. The others were right for his team but he was uncertain about this last one. Why was Miss Spencer so adamant?

'He'll be a great performer,' she said. 'Wait until you see him jump.'

There was no argument. Bill shrugged. 'If he can find his direction, maybe. But he's not got an idea of where he's going . . .'

Jonathan had just bumped into a Parkview student. The children around him were sniggering.

'Get off,' the boy commanded.

Jonathan's face was turning red. He wanted this whole thing to be over.

Since Miss Spencer's entry, the room had been transformed from a gloomy place to one of sunshine and light. The last traces of rain had disappeared from the window. There was an air of expectancy as those kids not called up waited for a future that hung in the balance.

Jonathan could hear snatches of Bill's final decision but he couldn't make sense of the words. His own failure was obvious. Whatever else, he must pass Miss Spencer with some dignity.

Then Mia was mouthing rudely at him again. She was already a success story. Why wouldn't she leave him alone?

'He's calling for you,' she said. 'Go on, hurry up.'

Jonathan couldn't move. He was frozen to the spot. Then he caught sight of Miss Spencer and she was beckoning him too. Her wave was graceful, as if for a moment she had taken over the role of Princess Aurora.

Mysteriously his feet began to carry him and Jonathan threw out his chest in the way that he found easy. He smiled and went towards her, almost running.

* * *

'D'you want some of this?'

Back in the changing room, one of the Parkview boys offered Jonathan a swig from his high-energy drink. The three from the same school had their street clothes on, their practice gear shoved carelessly into bags.

'Thanks,' Jonathan said.

He took the can and drank thirstily until the gas came back and hit him in the mouth.

The boy with the cheekbones stood over him. 'Did you get through?' He was checking his watch.

'Yes,' said Jonathan. His throat was hurting again and he wanted to be alone.

'Yo, I'm Tom,' said the boy.

The Viewpoint Academy students obviously spoke their own language.

The one with the shaved head remained silent.

The other, whose drink it was, had blond streaks through his dark hair and freckles. 'I'm Zak,' he said between gulps.

Jonathan was too exhausted to take anything more in and he was cold. The rickety bench he sat on was scratched with the legacy of previous names. Perhaps right now his bum covered somebody famous.

Tom had raised a fist into the air. 'Yo,' he said again.

A pencil could have rested on each of his cheekbones. Jonathan tried to be joyful. 'Hey,' he croaked.

Mia was swinging about in the passage. Mrs Nathan knelt on the floor, picking up tights and remnants from her daughter's make-up bag.

'Auditions are easy, Mum,' she sang and, as kids left the building, she called out appropriate comments to each one of them.

'Maybe next time,' Mia said to Kayla, who walked out hand in hand with a woman they didn't recognise.

The girl stared stubbornly ahead and didn't answer. Mrs Morrison wanted to smack her.

'Who would be in this business, eh?' said Mrs Nathan.

But she was elated, anyone could see that. Mia's mother would get involved like she always did, helping with costumes and mucking in generally.

Then Jonathan had appeared. 'Hello, Mum,' he said.

'Who's a lucky boy, then?' sang Mia in a high descant. She rubbed her hair at the top until it foamed outwards, framing her oval face. Her natural highlights were to be envied.

They were almost the last to leave, when from around the corner there was a sound of sobbing. Kayla appeared, not so tall now but shrunk into her shoulders and holding the same woman's hand. Her eyes were filling even as she walked.

'I'll never make it,' she cried, and then she cried more and couldn't speak at all.

The woman looked worried. 'Her mother was working so I brought her here,' she said. Her voice took on an undertone. 'Kayla wants an operation,' she whispered.

'What for?' asked Jonathan. He didn't like to see people crying, especially girls.

'To reduce her height,' said the woman. 'Isn't it awful?'

They left slowly, Kayla's sobs receding gradually into the distance.

Mia had begun to skip up and down. 'Fancy wanting an operation to make yourself shorter,' she blurted between jumps.

Her mother and Mrs Morrison exchanged glances.

Jonathan took Mia's arms and pinned them into his own. He was glad he had enough strength left. 'Why don't you ever shut up?' he asked.

Outside the building, water was running in a small current that made the ground soggy. The two drunks hadn't moved from their position but they were now lying down.

'Hello, son,' said the talkative one.

'Hi,' said Jonathan.

The air was murky.

'Anything for the homeless?' the tramp asked.

Jonathan could see filthy fingernails through the man's gloves. He felt into his back pocket and fished out the only coin he could find. It was the Euro. 'Here,' he said.

The tramp clasped his hand over the coin. 'Good luck to you son,' he said, and Jonathan wondered whether he could buy a hat one day to cover his few wisps of hair.

Jonathan had developed a temperature. Somehow the pantomime was no longer real and the audition only in his sub-conscious.

Lying in bed at home, Jonathan tried to imagine what he would be doing on stage. He was obviously going to be a sailor but when he imagined pulling ropes and sails, the technical feats seemed impossible. His eyes flickered restlessly.

Nureyev's poster had taken on muddy colours and his boots were objects of aggression.

Then his mother came in. 'Are you going to be all right, love?' she asked him. 'I've brought Barnaby in to see you for a short while.'

Mrs Morrison was weary herself and still had the prospect of breaking the news about *Sinbad* to Peter. She was not looking forward to it.

The guinea pig *tweak*ed between the red stripes of Jonathan's pyjamas. Jonathan stared at his mother as though he didn't recognise her. She had worry lines each side of her mouth.

'Mum,' he said. He was feeling drowsy at last. 'If I'm going to be a professional, I can't have holes in my tights.'

Mrs Morrison kissed him lightly on the top of his head. 'I'll come back for Barnaby,' she said.

Then the light was out. He wasn't sure whether she was still with him, but he was drifting now into that series of pink clouds that he always came to. With the guinea pig very still under his hands, Jonathan fell fast asleep.

Chapter Six

He had a dream. The three Parkview boys, dressed as cowboys, were galloping somewhere out in the West. Their horses drummed hooves into the plain and made the earth shake. They were after Jonathan. The shadow of a great lasso hung over him as he tried to get his own piebald moving. But Jonathan was on the wrong horse. Though he shook the reins and dug his spurs in desperately, his mount was a lazy beast and kept on stalling. Meanwhile, the Parkview gang drew closer. When the lasso caught him and pulled him off his saddle, his head hit the dusty ground and Jonathan lost consciousness. Coming to, Tom stood above him, strong and silent. He was an integral part of the landscape.

'You've lost your hat,' he said.

Jonathan was in bed for two days after that with a high temperature. When he wasn't sleeping, he read the five voyages of Sinbad and decided there and then that if he didn't make it as a dancer, he would become a diamond merchant. He liked the idea of hunting for jewels in exotic places, though not the bit where Sinbad got picked up in an eagle's talons on the second voyage. How was that going to happen in the pantomime? Jonathan wondered.

Mr Morrison brought him his food and his mother continued to work at the garden centre. She dropped in once or twice, her mobile clamped to her ear and dropping bits of soil on the stairs. Jonathan could tell that his mother was under pressure. That made two of them in the family!

'How's the invalid?' she asked on a late visit, breathless and windswept, as she peered round Jonathan's bedroom door. She could see his colour was improving.

'When are you coming home for longer than two minutes, Mum?' he asked.

'Dad's hopeless.'

Mrs Morrison laughed and as she did so, her expression became almost optimistic.

Then it died.

'Soon,' she said.

On the third day, Jonathan came downstairs on wobbly legs with a different sort of appetite. He didn't fancy scrambled eggs or chicken soup. He wanted something more substantial.

'Dad!' he shouted. 'I'm hungry.'

Mr Morrison didn't answer. He was in his study, which combined filing cabinets with his wife's latest magazines on water features and lilies from the Amazon. There were a couple of tarnished trophy cups from his rugby days on the mantelpiece, a floor to ceiling bookcase and the family desk weighted under papers.

The middle shelf of the bookcase held a series of leather-bound volumes entitled *Walking with Moorhouse*. Jonathan could just glimpse his father's qualifications in bold on the computer. They didn't seem to have moved on very much from his sporting activities at Durham.

Outside the window, trees were bare of all leaves and their branches hung abandoned in the weak morning light. Jonathan put his face to the glass and tried to make out the shape of Barnaby at his grill. He would have to bring him in for the winter.

Unexpectedly, he was lonely and aware of great

distances. His father hadn't mentioned *Sinbad*. It was as though the audition had never taken place, the event a figment of his imagination, and where ballet dancers such as himself waited in limbo.

'What are you doing, Dad?' Jonathan asked. He traced the curvature of a twig on a windowpane.

Peter was reading one of his many job applications without interest. The fact that it was for an advertising campaign on a new EU initiative did not inspire. There was a lot going on in Brussels.

'Learning about Belgium,' said Mr Morrison. He supposed in a way that was true. A draught under the door had shifted his papers into an unwieldy collection.

Jonathan was now standing in front of his father. Their eyes met, ready for confrontation. Peter saw the same dark pools of rebellion that had characterised his own adolescence and sighed.

'We've had a call from Mrs Humphries,' he said. 'She's unhappy with your progress and wants you to have private lessons.'

'Can't!' said Jonathan. He roamed his father's face anxiously. 'Dad, did Mum tell you about *Sinbad*?' Jonathan was on the point of jigging again.

Yes, Mr Morrison knew about the pantomime. The

fact that his wife had kept the audition from him still rankled. Now Jonathan had been offered a job as a *fait accompli* without even discussing the issue.

'There are only four boys in the show and I get a salary, Dad,' he said.

That was another thing. Jonathan would be earning more money than his father's income support over the next few weeks.

Mr Morrison leant forward to show that he was serious. 'I don't want you in the theatre,' he said in a low voice. 'It's very unstable. You'll spend over half your dancing life out of work.'

Jonathan wanted to say something horrible. After all, his dad had been out of work for half a year. He longed suddenly for the sound of Mum's key in the door, for the smell of the light scent that always accompanied her.

Mr Morrison broke the silence. 'Mrs Humphries tells me you don't concentrate. In fact, the general consensus seems to be that you are in one long daydream from the moment you arrive at school to the moment you get out.'

'Everybody has troubles with Hugs Bugs, Dad,' said Jonathan. 'We're all afraid of catching her germs because she never stops coughing. Alex thinks she's got a bad disease.'

No wonder they weren't learning anything, Jonathan thought. Sam's mother had sent him a dozen linen handkerchiefs from Bloomingdale's in New York and some of the boys in the class were using them as gas masks. Sam never got into trouble though, even when he answered Hugs Bugs through his handkerchief. He was too good at maths.

There was the drone of an aeroplane on the horizon. Jonathan craned his neck with difficulty as he followed the thin trail of silver up and out towards another country. Only the clouds hung listless now above the garden. A lump came back into his throat. Jonathan would like to have been on that plane, above a warm sea and heading for Bassorah. The place where treasure seekers gathered . . .

'This is exactly what I mean!'

Mr Morrison's voice had entered Jonathan's subconscious to jar against him.

'You're not listening again.'

'I'm trying,' Jonathan said. He wanted to reassure his dad, so added, 'The council has rules about people my age working in the theatre.' Jonathan hadn't finished. 'Mia says we have to be looked after all the time.'

'That's going to be a further reason why your mother is never here,' said Mr Morrison.

The phone was ringing from his desk. Jonathan waited for his father to pick up the receiver.

'It's Alex,' Mr Morrison said with none of his usual friendliness. 'He says he has left three messages on your mobile.'

'Hi,' said Jonathan, taking the phone. Why couldn't be alone to take his call?

'Hi,' answered Alex.

The weather must have hit him too. Everyone was in a depression, Jonathan decided.

'What's happening?' he asked. 'Why aren't you at school?' There was a lot of noise at the back of the phone, as if someone was hoovering.

'My dad's left home,' said Alex. His tone was nasal.

Jonathan glanced at his own father who had gone back to reading small print.

'Mine nearly has,' he said. 'Come on over.'

Alex arrived at the house in the late afternoon. He had brought his electric toothbrush and his football with him.

'Fancy a game, Mr Morrison?' he asked immediately.

He was already dribbling with the ball on the kitchen tiles. Then Mr Morrison took it up in a balancing act on his head that made Alex whistle.

'Wow,' he said.

There was an affinity between them. Jonathan might as well have been invisible. He had never been part of the sports set and this was one moment when he wanted to be. His father was smiling.

They all ate pizza in front of the TV afterwards. Peter lit the fire and three of them sat sprawled over cushions that had lost their spring. Alex had red eyes. Jonathan could recognise a trauma.

'You've got tomato sauce on your chin,' he said instead to Alex, who stuck out his tongue and let it curl like an anticipating snake.

'Ugh . . .' said Jonathan.

The boys laughed, but not too noisily. Peter's head had fallen sideways and he was dozing as he always did at the start of the evening news. When Mrs Morrison came in late, she felt the warmth of a room that was almost claustrophobic.

On a satellite channel, Jonathan and Alex followed a bent US detective's drive through Miami. As he pulled into a greasy diner, two men came out through the doors to meet him.

Alex yawned. 'That guy's wicked,' he said. The football lay still between his trainers.

Mrs Morrison was too tired to mind the strong smell of pastrami pizza. Her arms ached from wheeling trolley loads of bamboo posts from a van to the garden centre.

'Alex is staying the night, Mum,' said Jonathan. 'His dad's left home.'

Mrs Morrison looked across at the man she had married for better or for worse and saw only his slack jaw in repose. It wasn't a pretty sight. The two boys were watching her.

'He can sleep in my room,' Jonathan said.

His mother sat down between them with a bump, and drew Alex close to her. He seemed to want her there. Then he patted his knees with both hands.

'Off you go,' Mrs Morrison said lightly. 'You've both got school tomorrow.'

Jonathan pulled the duvet off the spare room bed and brought it next to his own. Neither of them could sleep when the time came.

'I'm too hot,' said Alex.

He had thrown off his cover and was kicking it at the same time. Jonathan could hear raised voices through the wall, his father's verbal assault drowning his mother's responses.

'Your mum's cool,' Alex said. 'Mine keeps breaking our cups.'

'Is she clumsy?' asked Jonathan. He wiggled his toes and found new areas of coolness in which to place his feet. He was very aware of his dancer's body and the importance of repose.

'She does it on purpose,' said Alex, 'and my dad says he'll have to win the lottery to replace all the china she's broken.'

The voices next door had gone quiet. Jonathan stared unblinkingly into the night until he could no longer hear Alex tossing and turning.

There was nothing else to do, he reflected, but become famous. He didn't want to get married or sit for ever over sums that were incomprehensible. One day Jonathan was going to a place where lights would use up electricity on the letters of his name.

Chapter Seven

A week after the audition, Bill Jones and Reg were seated in the window of The Kovalam restaurant. They were not far from the Albany Theatre where *Sinbad The Sailor* posters advertised the forthcoming production.

The Albany was a recent addition to the town and audiences had come in droves since its opening to enjoy drama locally. *Sinbad* was the first pantomime to be performed there and Bill was pleased about that. At least his billing was visible, which was more than could be said for Reggie's. As musical director of the show, Reginald Faner was listed further down and in green. But Reggie knew his place. The partnership between them had always been fostered under the conditions of Bill's hierarchy.

At three-fifteen in the afternoon, the shopping precinct was busy. People browsed down the lines of lingerie and fashion boutiques before moving on to supermarket chains. Others sat at the mall café, enjoying hot drinks and the pale, wintry sunshine.

The Indian restaurant was located opposite a square and, in summer, flowerbeds spilt across paths leading to the town's memorial. Today there was something going on. From Bill and Reggie's window, an interesting spectacle was taking place in full view of them. Several men were unloading a very tall Christmas tree from a forklift truck and moving it to the centre of the square.

'That's going to take all day,' said Bill. He was immersed in the mechanics of crossing ropes directed by a foreman.

'Like our lunch,' muttered Reg.

He had finished his curry and already felt the customary burning sensation in the pit of his stomach. Reg spent a lot of time when he was out with Bill regretting his choice of menu. He couldn't bear the sight of their half-eaten dishes. The *sag gosht* and lamb *pasanda* were beginning to congeal and an empty bottle of pinot grigio bobbed up and down in a bucket of melted ice.

Bill signalled to the only waiter left to serve them.

'Another bottle,' he said.

The waiter nodded. He went to the back of the restaurant and disappeared through a swing door.

'I'm relaxing,' said Bill.

His interest returned to the tree, which was tilting unexpectedly to the right. A couple more men had joined the others and there were shouts as the truck manoeuvred round and backed into the main road. Traffic that converged there before routing off to other areas of the town had come to a halt.

'Well, we've got our cast organised,' said Bill, still contemplating. 'The only question mark is over Alfred and whether or not he is going to be free to play the Caliph.' He rubbed the gold chain round his neck like a talisman.

'Of course he'll be free,' answered Reg. 'He couldn't bear to let anyone else do the part. I mean, Alfred *is* the Caliph, isn't he?'

Bill found the thickness of Reggie's steel-rimmed glasses disconcerting. They made his eyes pop, as if he was mad. Lately, Reg had been very edgy. They needed to make time for each other . . . pace themselves instead of covering the length and breadth of the country whenever a job beckoned.

Bill Jones didn't like to admit that he was past his prime. He had spent years as principal dancer with the Zadoos and taken top billing in more summer seasons than he cared to remember. Now he directed regional shows, including pantomimes and, luckily for Reggie, had made a bit of a come back.

But *Sinbad* was going to be their last pantomime for a while. Frankly, Bill was suffering from burn out and he couldn't take Reg's dire warnings about their health on the road any longer.

The waiter returned, opening their second bottle of wine.

'No hurry,' said Bill, 'we want to enjoy ourselves.'

The golden shade of his glass made him mellow and he decided that he could stay here comfortably for another hour at least.

'Better be careful,' Reg said, 'we'll have to get a taxi to drive us home.'

The waiter stood still, momentarily in some world beyond them. He seemed to be a man of great sorrow. Then, without warning, he leant across the two diners and peered intently at the outside view.

'Oh my God,' he said.

Bill and Reg turned again to the window. Somebody

was calling out as a man ran towards the left side of the tree. He was followed by three more. A loud snap broke through the proceedings and two of the topmost branches keeled over and dropped to the ground. The rope was quickly taken up to compensate and a group worked to bring the Christmas tree finally upright. It shuddered on the spot in flimsy distress, missing the weight of upper foliage.

'Shame,' said Reggie as the lorry began to move away.

Pedestrians had stopped in front of the square to follow the action. The foreman took his cap off and scratched his head. Bill drained his glass. He didn't want to be at the scene of any failure, even somebody else's.

'My stomach's on the heave ho,' Reg said. He was always frail.

Bill took some cash out of his wallet. 'Come on,' he ordered, 'your guts are giving me a headache.'

A few miles away at Northside, Jonathan was suffering from claustrophobia. He had eight minutes in which to finish his assessment test and there was still the back page to do. Mrs Humphries sat at the top table facing the boys. She was dressed for show in pink cardigan, purple skirt and a stab of scarlet lipstick. The lipstick had gone over the edges of her mouth and when she smiled, her teeth were luminous through the red alert.

Mrs Humphries was in full favour of National Curriculum Maths Key Stage 2. She wanted to encourage her boys to think the same way too. But in Jonathan's class, there were only Sam and Marcus who did.

Another form's work was being marked. Jonathan could see from his position a series of ticks flicking down the margins. They were painful to him. His next problem concerned part of a timetable and the arrival of a train in Domley. But which train was it?

Jonathan looked down at the columns of hours and minutes, all of which had possibilities, and he didn't have a clue. As for how long the journey took, that was a question way beyond his parameters of knowledge.

Jonathan could see Sam leaning back dangerously on one leg of his chair and yawning. He had obviously finished ages ago. Marcus too had crossed his arms and was staring at the ceiling. It wasn't fair. Why did they find maths so easy?

Jonathan returned to his timetable again and decided that the town, Domley, had a pretty boring ring to its name. Anyway, he thought to himself, when he was fully trained and working, he wouldn't go anywhere by train. Nureyev would never have travelled that way between galas. He would have flown in an aeroplane. Or gone by taxi. Jonathan brightened. Taxis were easy. His mum had taken one with him once a long time ago. She had given the driver a twenty-pound note. The driver had worked out the change.

'Two minutes,' said Mrs Humphries.

There was a groan along the lines of those still working. Jonathan decided to stop early. He didn't see the point of carrying on and getting even more muddled. He wished he had some chewing gum. Hugs Bugs had started to wheeze, which meant she was probably excited. She was patting her chest now and her bosoms were moving like two big car bumpers. Then she began to sneeze.

'Papers in,' she said with a blustery voice.

The signal for action was clear. Sam took a well-pressed linen handkerchief from his desk and wound it round the lower half of his face.

'This is mission control,' he croaked through the mask.

At Sam's signal, a mass of other handkerchiefs appeared as the rest of the boys followed suit. Then they were all part of the same gang. Hugs Bugs was coughing hard. She hadn't even noticed.

For a moment Jonathan shut his eyes and imagined the snow.

Mrs Morrison waited by the school exit gates and thought about her increasingly heavy work schedule. How was she going to organise everything during the *Sinbad* run? There wouldn't be any help from her husband, that was for sure. They were at odds not only over the panto but every home issue it seemed.

She shifted her feet through a pile of autumn leaves. They were turning to mulch. Mrs Morrison sighed and looked through the playground fence almost automatically. Children were running helter skelter under the lights, pulling on satchels and screaming. Jonathan came out slowly behind the others. The way his head was down gave him away. Mrs Morrison knew at once he must have had a bad time in maths.

'Hi, Mum,' he said.

His heavy fringe fell over his eyes. They were darker than usual. Mrs Morrison squeezed the stocky figure of her son very tightly.

'Ouch,' he said, moving away from her. 'You've torn your trousers at the knee,' he remarked. Then he smiled. She was never going to change.

Mrs Morrison had bent to survey the damage and somehow money was spilling out of her handbag.

'You're useless, Mum,' Jonathan called.

He had gone ahead again and was busy hopping to the car.

Mrs Morrison gathered her change and shook some leaves from her clothes. 'Wait for me,' she said, and was glad that he couldn't hear the catch in her voice.

Jonathan had enough to worry about in his life right now.

At home, there was an envelope on the drawing room mantelpiece addressed to Jonathan Morrison. It was formally propped up between the china shepherdess and a pot plant. Jonathan took the letter down carefully.

Inside was confirmation of his place in the show and also a rehearsal schedule. Underlined was the stipulation that children must be accompanied by an adult at all times and something about the Young Persons Act. After wishing the cast a happy and successful season, the letter was signed in a flowery scrawl by Bill Jones, director of *Sinbad The Sailor*.

Jonathan gave a whoop of delight and kissed his mum. 'This is it,' he said and he did a little jig until she couldn't help but laugh.

'Go and feed Barnaby,' she said. 'I've got some phoning to do.'

Jonathan cut up a cucumber into big slices and took them over to the guinea pig's box. Barnaby was hungry. He was gnashing his own bed made up of Mr Morrison's newspaper and had strips of print between his teeth.

Jonathan wanted to talk to his dad, but the hut was dark and there was no sign of him anywhere. Outside, the cold was intense and night had come without him even noticing. A fine layer of white frost covered the undergrowth and the branches of every tree. Jonathan could recognise their beauty. It was a pity, he thought, that his appreciation of nature was not a talent yet recognised through school and the National Curriculum.

Chapter Eight

At *nine forty-five a.m.* on November twenty-fifth, Mrs
Morrison left her son at The Cellars with Mrs Nathan
for his first day of rehearsals. As he waved a stiff goodbye,
Jonathan's nerves got the better of him.

'Wish me luck, Mum,' he said, and there was a
grimness in him that she did not recognise.

Jonathan hardly acknowledged the same tramp in
the doorway. His mind was on other things. For once,
his mother thought happily, she had brought him to a
destination on time.

Jonathan had prepared for this moment for so long
that the reality of it all took him by surprise. He had
difficulty changing his clothes, and his body felt stiff and

awkward. The ballet shoes that he put on had the texture of cardboard and his fringe stuck up in the air. Everyone else had changed already. Why couldn't he behave more like a dancer? he wondered.

When he came into the studio, Mia was already leaning back against the *barre* in a way that he found quite disgusting. She wore a bright blue leotard with tights, and her hair was woven once again into a thick plait. Jonathan wanted to tell her to disappear. Instead, he decided to get on with a few exercises.

The boys had already begun. He put his feet into position and executed a small *grand battement*. As his right leg came off the floor, Jonathan watched Tom bend his knees with faultless turnout.

The Cellars' former disco area was now the main practice room. There were mock roman columns covered in graffiti and the remains of a bar took up one entire wall. An empty bottle of gin lay discarded in an alcove. The lighting was too bright and made the room very hot. Out of the twelve kids present, only five in total were from the Neptune Arts Centre. The remainder were from two different theatre schools, including the Parkview.

When Miss Spencer arrived alone, Mia stood close to Jonathan. 'She's teaching us the entire choreography,'

Jonathan's Leap

she said. 'It's a shame we haven't got Bill because he's more modern.' She gave a frown, plotting how to become invaluable to the production.

'Bill's an ex-jazz dancer,' Jonathan said. 'He's not got a background in ballet.' Mrs Nathan had told him that. The Nathan family knew everything.

'We're just not doing ballet,' Mia mouthed.

Before he could respond, she was being ushered away from him and into the crowd of girls.

Miss Spencer absently lay her hands on the top of her head. Her bun was more sharply defined than usual, her normally pale faced touched with rouge. She waited patiently for the children to stop talking.

'We are going to work on the Underwater Ballet,' she said. 'This sequence comes at the end of the first act where the Old Man of the Sea creates a terrible storm.'

Mia was pushing forward. 'Is the Princess on stage here?' she asked. Mia had big ideas. She swung her hips round as if she had an imaginary hula hoop.

'Shhh . . .' said Zak of the streaky hair and freckles. He didn't like her.

Miss Spencer's voice was deliberately slow. 'Will you please listen, all of you,' she said.

She was starting to move across the floor now, her

71

arms moving fast and with lunges first to the right and then to the left.

'Follow me,' she called.

Jonathan tried to mark directly behind her but Tom had got there first. He was taller than all the others too. It was difficult to see.

As if by magic, music was coming from the direction of one of the pillars. Jonathan realised that the pianist was playing something important like a concerto. Then he caught a glimpse of Reggie's outsize coat billowing from each side of the pillar. He was making a noisy din around lower C that promised battle.

'That's just what we need, Reggie,' puffed Miss Spencer. She had come to a halt in the middle of the room, holding fingers close to her heart. 'On to our confrontation between good and evil. We have Tom here . . .'

There were exclamations of surprise from the other children.

'This is the big fight between the Princess's guide and the Old Man of the Sea, who is mortally wounded.'

Jonathan interrupted. 'But what about the Roc? I hope he gets killed.'

The Roc was a horrific bird with an appetite.

Miss Spencer sensed Jonathan's worries. 'The Old

Man and the Roc represent evil and you can guess who comes out top,' she said. 'All's well in the end.'

The kids thought about this.

'What about Princess Pearl?' asked Mia. She wouldn't give up.

Miss Spencer folded her hands around her waist as if to demonstrate how small she really was. 'We're having a dancer from the Moncrieff Ballet,' she said. 'But she won't be with us until a few days before the show opens.'

There was another gasp from the children. Mia's eyes had gone wide with speculation.

'Let's go again,' Miss Spencer said firmly.

Reggie played some more very loud chords in the bass clef.

After this, nobody spoke.

Miss Spencer was choreographing as she went along. She covered the ground quickly with steps that grew into jumps and then slowed back again into walks.

'I want the feeling of another world under the sea. You are sprites with an ethereal quality,' she said, puffing.

'What does ethereal mean?' asked one of the girls who stood shuffling at the back.

Mia clicked her tongue in contempt. 'We're fairies, stupid,' she said.

Jonathan's feet were tired. This choreography business was serious and he was having trouble remembering the sequence. Amy had a sad face, but Jonathan saw that she was looking at him.

'A little more energy, dear,' Miss Spencer said in her direction.

Tom and the guy with the shaved head were strides ahead. Jonathan wondered when they would be able to sit down.

During the lunch break, he ate a ham and cheese baguette in the canteen with Mia and Amy. Mrs Nathan was in charge of them and had spent the hours so far knitting at the back of the rehearsal room. Jonathan could have eaten a whole chicken. He wanted more. He hadn't realised that there would be so much to think about but when he saw Amy stuffing herself, he felt a lot better.

'There's going to be a real ballet dancer playing Princess Pearl,' Mia told her mother.

Mrs Nathan smiled and went on with her knitting. 'Terrific,' she said. It wouldn't be long before her daughter was a princess in her own right.

Mia rolled her eyes. 'Everyone's jealous of me at school because I'm the only one in a pantomime,' she said in a high voice.

Amy was rubbing her stomach. 'I feel sick,' she groaned.

Jonathan couldn't see any sign of the boys. He felt that it was important to be in their presence even if he wasn't one of them. Perhaps they were in the studio.

When he came up the stairs to find out, Jonathan heard the music first. Through the open door he saw Tom, who had the appearance of a soloist already. His position was close to the floor where Jonathan waited for several seconds.

'Now your two turns, and then up . . .' called Miss Spencer.

She was there in the middle of the room, half shaping Tom's movements alongside him. He spun in the light with a great energy.

'Into the *jetes*!' Miss Spencer cried. She was springing like the young dancer she must once have been. Tom pulled upright and ran into a series of leaps that made his legs split wide open in the air. He was holding each move for seconds, almost as though he were primed for a video. His style was brilliant and frightening to Jonathan all at the same time.

He stood in the doorway, not daring to move.

'Pick up the sword, Tom,' ordered Miss Spencer.

She was still running. The pins from her bun were scattering onto the floor. Tom picked up an imaginary sword and slashed his fist through the air. As the music grew to a full crescendo, he dug into his opponent. This final action lasted for ages. Rather too long, Jonathan decided.

When he had finished, Tom wiped the sweat from his face. He wanted her approval.

'Good,' she said softly, 'you've got the tension right, but we just need to work a bit more on the spins.'

The boy had turned fully again into the light. Jonathan felt quite helpless in the presence of such talent. Not only did Tom have the cheekbones and the right build for a dancer, he was as confident as any member of a company. Jonathan might have the higher jump, but this other boy looked like the real thing. A soloist!

Tom passed him in the passage. 'Yo,' he said casually. He was slim but muscular. Tom jabbed at Jonathan's shoulders as if to emphasise his more flabby structure. 'Just pacing through the first of my solos,' he said.

'Are there more?' asked Jonathan. He had that familiar lump in his throat again.

Tom had leapt towards the stairs in a single bound. 'Only two,' he called before disappearing.

Jonathan came back into the doorway of the studio where Miss Spencer had inserted another CD into her player. Strains of violin and cello were filling the space between them. Her hair had now fallen completely away from her bun and hung loose. With her back to him, she wasn't the Miss Spencer Jonathan knew any more. She was moving her arms quite differently in a sort of embrace and then beating them as if they were wings.

Watching her, Jonathan wondered who the missing partner might have been. He wished it was him. Perhaps Miss Spencer was practising a bit from The Dying Swan. There was something so pathetic about the piece, she made Jonathan quite sad.

Gradually she completed a circle, only to shake her whole body in the throes of death.

Jonathan didn't dare do anything. He knew that this performance of Miss Spencer's was a private thing. Suddenly she keeled over, moaning and clasping her stomach. It was as if the light had never been there.

He couldn't stay silent any longer. 'Are you all right, Miss Spencer?' he asked.His voice echoed in the silence. He wanted to hold her for a second so that she would be better, but she was beyond his help.

'I'll be fine in a minute,' she gasped.

Gradually Miss Spencer shook herself free of whatever had given her pain. Her face was clear again. Jonathan saw his teacher then as she always was, in control and serene.

'Not a word,' she said quietly. 'Now call the others up. We have another hour to work.'

When Jonathan came back to the canteen, he saw Mia surrounded by the cast of kids. They were admiring a pendant around her neck and Jonathan didn't like the way she was showing it off with one long fingernail hooked behind the chain.

'It's from a shop in Madrid,' she murmured.

'We've got to go upstairs again,' said Jonathan. He had serious things to consider.

'Oh no,' sighed Mia. She went on flicking at her pendant, but nobody was paying her attention now.

'Time to go, everyone!' shouted the boy with the shaved head. 'And I'm Cameron by the way, guys.'

Jonathan let Cameron take over. He was still thinking about Miss Spencer. Without wanting to be, he was in a conspiracy with her that he would have to keep to himself.

Chapter Nine

Whilst Jonathan rehearsed his first steps for the Underwater Ballet, Peter Morrison found himself waiting to see his bank manager in the centre of town.

For half an hour now, he had sat facing the foreign exchange counter and been informed that the manager was no longer with them. This was worrying news.

With Mr Morrison's overdraft running into four figures, he needed a sympathetic ear.

Mr Morrison was struck, not for the first time, by the many customers about him who were experiencing a busy day. He wondered how many of them were like him and out of work. Everyone had a mobile in their hand and someone to talk to.

Having been made redundant, Peter Morrison felt that his phone had gone the same way. Even his own son never rang him and Charmian's texts were usually requests for him to go supermarket shopping.

'Mr Morrison?'

He was being ushered into an office by a young woman whose high heels clawed into the pile of carpet as she strode ahead.

She closed the door. 'Please,' she said, 'have a seat.'

The room was uncomfortably warm, and adorned with a rubber plant that had grown just short of the ceiling.

'We're here to discuss the last extension to your overdraft, is that right, Mr Morrison?' the woman asked. She wore glasses and when her eyes made contact with Peter's, they were magnified and the colour of Mediterranean blue.

'That's right,' he said.

He tried to smile at the woman but her response was to look through him. She was young enough to be his daughter and although they had never met, her grasp of his affairs was instant. Only twelve months ago, Peter had been well into the black with enough set aside for a family trip to South America.

There was something about the way she inclined

her head at him. The quizzical gaze. As the woman adjusted papers in front of her and came back to meet his brief responses, Peter Morrison felt a desire to leave the room.

She didn't care that he was responsible for a family or begin to understand the precariousness of his situation.

Yet she reminded him of someone . . . that same oval shape to her face . . . the air of fragility receding yet again . . . his pain at her removal. With the shock of the new, Mr Morrison was remembering a figure from his past whom he could never obliterate.

She was talking again, about the details of a business plan that he must deliver a week from today without fail. But the room swam around him. The rubber plant seemed to take up all Mr Morrison's air, its tangled mess of leaves ready to gather him in.

'If you have any problems, don't hesitate to call me,' the woman said.

She was standing now and extending her hand to shake his own. Mr Morrison stared at the business card she had given him, showing her name and status as customer support manager. The woman's eyes were no longer so piercingly blue. She was smaller than she had first appeared, her authority already diminishing. Perhaps she too was going back to some grubby desk and a bunch of useless emails.

He had credit again and Mr Morrison's exit from the bank made him reckless. He wanted to surprise his wife. In the days when they had been well off, he would take time out to buy new perfumes in the nearest store to his agency. He had got to know the girls behind the counter.

'Try this one, Mr Morrison,' they would tease him.

Eventually he had discovered essences containing bergamot and pomegranate. He could breathe in those different scents now. Mr Morrison had a longing for Charmian to be next to him and in clothes not worn at the garden centre.

Mr Morrison found himself whistling unexpectedly as he walked by Boots. The bustling of sales assistants and customers drew him beyond the glossy window displays. He was surprised to hear 'Hark the Herald Angels Sing' through the loudspeakers and to see so much Christmas packaging. Christmas already . . . Mr Morrison was glad that his overdraft would just about carry him through the festivities.

Again he thought of Charmian there in the middle of other shoppers . . . her rapt concentration . . . her enjoyment at buying the items they had once taken for granted. Jonathan too who, like his mother, could never make up his mind. The interminable waiting for them in a shop . . . the croissants at a café afterwards. Amongst the crowds in the chemist's, Mr Morrison was aware of being lonely.

'Can I help you?' a sales assistant asked him.

He held a box of Chanel No. 5 in his hands without knowing it. The assistant wore too much make-up. Her cheeks glowed under translucent powder and the uniform she had on was covered with specks of gold dust.

Peter gave her the box. 'I want this gift wrapped,' he said.

Once out of the main mall, Mr Morrison walked left and downhill from the mass of pedestrians. He came soon to the bottom, and to a line of alms cottages with prim lawns that he hadn't known existed.

At the end of the next street stood a small pub with no discernable features. Mr Morrison went in and ordered a lager. He needed a drink. There were other men here too, spread on stools, unshaved, anonymous like himself. Some read newspapers. Others stared vacantly through frosted windows. The landlord leant forward over the bar. He had given up on his crossword and sipped unobtrusively from a cup of coffee.

'Been buying for the missus?' he asked with his eyes on Peter's shiny red-papered box and yawning. 'The season comes round too quick, that's what I always say.'

Mr Morrison didn't want conversation. He wished to remain silent amongst regulars who understood the need to be alone.

The landlord went on. 'Now we've got a bloomin' pantomime an all,' he said. 'My kids are already on tenterhooks to see it but they'll have to go with their mum.'

A short, fat woman had come to stand next to him. She put an arm around his back. 'Give over,' she said. 'It's Christmas and all children like the panto. You used to, if you can remember.'

'Another lager, please,' said Mr Morrison.

The landlord looked down on his wife with a smile and chuckled. 'Marion's been in enough of them, haven't you, love?'

He was tickling her cardigan that stretched over a lace-collared blouse. The buttons had prised open at the top to reveal her mottled chest. For a moment, she was not with them but far away and experiencing some glamour in her past.

'Famous as Dick Whittington at the Tynegate

Hippodrome,' the landlord continued. 'It was her legs I first fell in love with.'

They were both laughing now. Mr Morrison tried to imagine a slimline Marion striding across the stage in tights.

'Good luck to you both,' he said. 'I'll have one more beer before I go.'

Mr Morrison was unaware of how he got home or the length of time it took him. On the way, he concentrated on what he was going to say to Charmian. Life had not been easy for her either, although she seemed to have taken to her gardening stints like a duck to water. His wife was working too hard. He would give her his present and she would respond with affection and surprise . . . then Mr Morrison could tell her how much he missed her.

There was a smell of tomato sauce cooking as he entered the house. His feet were unsteady. 'Damn,' he said to himself. Mr Morrison had the impression that he was tipsy and hoped very much that Jonathan wasn't around. With any luck, he would be rehearsing.

'Darling!'

His wife had come out from the kitchen and was staring at him as she might a stranger. Her hair clung to her forehead from the heat, a loose curl just tracing the base of her earlobe. Mr Morrison felt such a rush of emotion, he could hardly contain himself.

'I've bought you something,' he said.

As she took the package and fumbled with the wrapping, he wanted to help her. Charmian was irritable. Mr Morrison could see that when she had opened the box.

'It's sweet of you, darling . . .' She hesitated. 'But please don't spend money on me. We're only just getting by . . .' Mrs Morrison patted Peter on the cheek. 'How did you get on at the bank?' she asked.

He watched her. 'I love you,' Peter said. His left leg had begun to tremble violently.

Mrs Morrison was already turning again towards the kitchen. 'You've been drinking,' she said without a backward glance.

'They've agreed an extension to my overdraft,' Peter called. He couldn't tell her that it was his last.

Why wouldn't she stay and tell him that they were going to be all right? He wanted reassurance, to kiss her face many times as he had done a long time ago in their former life.

He must see to his business plan. Rectify the situation.

With difficulty, Mr Morrison made his way to the study and brought up a particular file on his computer. Then he sat at his desk. There were various captions over a dozen pages, headings in bold and suggested marketing outlets.

Mr Morrison began to read his way through a proposal written by a French fisheries bureaucrat. He was aware that he was going to have to navigate an EU debt crisis as well as his own.

He tried to write a few words on paper, but his pen kept wobbling. The letters were ragged and made no sense to him at all. Mr Morrison's head began to drop down. His mouth slackened for the first snore and the struggle was over. A minute later, he had fallen fast asleep.

Chapter Ten

Jonathan was confused. He wasn't just a dancer in *Sinbad*. He also had words to say and songs to sing that made his previous Neptune Arts shows seem like very small productions. Bill had given scripts to all the kids and Jonathan spent every spare moment learning his lines. He was on stage more often than not: as a sailor, a water sprite, a merchant and also as one of the courtiers to King Hassan of Morocco. There was a doubling up on parts.

The leads were rehearsing separately for a few days so that the children could learn the full dance routines without interruption. They would soon join up together but until then any continuity was non-existent.

Miss Spencer drove them on. Every number had to be exactly right. Besides the Underwater Ballet and the Traders' Serenade, there was a drunken sailors' hornpipe, which made Jonathan dizzy even without the boat.

To his great annoyance, Jonathan found that Mia was usually placed as his opposite number and had taken on her characterisations with no extra prodding from Bill Jones. Bill liked Mia. She was always one step ahead. She knew where she was in the script before anyone else and had a habit of coming in early.

Jonathan felt unhappy with his mother. Apart from driving him to The Cellars and back, she hadn't helped him any more than necessary – just fifteen minutes so far to test him on his words!

The rhyme from the sailors' opening chorus still escaped him.

'Beef the sail and drop the anchor,' he mumbled through his toast and peanut butter two weeks later.

There were expressions here he had never heard of. Jonathan tried not to look at the page directly in front of him. But what on earth was the next line?

'Eat your breakfast, love,' Mrs Morrison said.

She was cramming the dishwasher with extra plates despite her husband's warning not to. An ominous noise vibrated through the sink unit when she pressed the *on* button.

Jonathan's lips continued to move silently.

'When do you get home tonight?' his mother asked. Mrs Nathan was chauffeur and minder for the day.

'When Mia can be bothered to get changed,' said Jonathan.

With the Nathans so big on wardrobe, the surprise was that they got anywhere at all. He wished his mum was a bit more into showbiz. Then she might understand how difficult it was wearing the same five T-shirts that had already been seen by the cast.

Jonathan understood that the production had a wardrobe mistress so he wouldn't have to worry about his costumes. Otherwise, what would he have done? Mum's last effort had been a ghost's tunic that was cut too small at the neck. Jonathan's glands had been sore for a whole week after that.

Mrs Morrison wiped the area around the table free of breadcrumbs. Her actions were mechanical. She had an inventory of new tools to put together for work and she still had orders to place for the spring. A new girl had come into the garden centre as a work experience placement and had left with grumbling appendicitis after a week. Mrs Morrison was suffering from lack of sleep. Peter had started to snore again. Last night, in desperation Mrs Morrison had hit him with her pillow. Then, when he stopped breathing, she hit him again and he had carried on just the same.

There was a hooting from outside.

'Mrs Nathan is here,' she said.

What a relief she didn't have to drive Jonathan. Peter hadn't left his bed yet and she would have to get him up before her departure. Jonathan was scrambling to get ready. With his tote bag and rucksack over his shoulder, he took his wrapped lunch from the fridge at a run. His mouth was still full. He couldn't say goodbye.

The shock of brilliant sunshine outside almost stopped Jonathan in his tracks. He was glad to be in the light, but the intense cold made him gasp and breathe out pockets of fog.

As he came closer to Mrs Nathan's car, he saw Mia next to her mother, wearing a sparkly jumper under her jacket. Her hair was hanging thick and loose.

'Hi,' he said as he got into the back seat.

It was covered in dog hairs. Just his luck. His cords would be ruined by the end of the drive.

Mrs Nathan was never lost for conversation. 'How's

everything going, Jonathan?' she asked as she drove off with a jolt.

'OK,' he said. He wasn't going to tell her any more. There were potholes in the road.

'Slow down, Mum, you're going too fast,' said Mia. Her heavy head of hair swung with the movement of the car.

'I think you're all marvellous,' continued Mrs Nathan.

Jonathan started to count the hairs that were collecting on his trousers.

Mia had her hands in a position of prayer. She was straining the backs of them until the knuckles cracked. Then she repeated the action.

'Another day working with the professionals,' Mrs Nathan said brightly.

Jonathan didn't know what she meant. Mia must have given her the low-down that they weren't there.

The opening chorus continued to haunt him.

Mia was still clicking her fingers.

'Don't do that, dear,' said Mrs Nathan. She wasn't a tall person and peered through the bottom of her windscreen rather than at the road ahead.

Mia hummed one note with perfect control of her diaphragm. Jonathan managed two lines from his verse as a silent accompaniment.

Mia broke off. 'You're indicating right and turning left, Mum.'

The car was heading straight for a series of cones that partitioned off road works. They were all in a slow-motion film now. Jonathan wondered at Mrs Nathan's accuracy. The whole lot of them were coming down one by one, like bowling pins in an alley.

Mia's mother stopped the car. 'Jonathan . . .' she said. She was appealing to him in her rear-view mirror. Her eyes had gone a bit pink and she seemed to be moist around the nose. 'Could you help me, dear?' she asked.

This time, they were late for rehearsal. The boys and girls already present were marking places as the traders at the opening of Act Two.

Bill was not in a good mood. 'What time do you call this?' he asked as Jonathan and Mia tried to creep in unnoticed.

Bill wore one those full floral Hawaiian shirts that Jonathan's father still liked to put on in the privacy of his own home. It was no comfort to Jonathan. Even worse, there was some new song in progress. Reg was at the piano and tinkering with a few notes.

Mia had removed her sparkly jumper to display a

purple all-in-one tights and leotard. Then she brandished one arm on the *barre*, confident of changing Bill's mood. Mia didn't have to work at stage presence.

'Jonathan had to put cones back in the road,' she said, pouting her lips.

Jonathan saw how Bill gazed at Mia with amused tolerance, as if noting her potential. He might as well not have been there at all.

The other kids were working on a routine. Jonathan slipped to the back and joined them. 'Have I missed much?' he whispered.

Cameron and Zak were teamed up together, in close and uncomfortable tandem.

'Zak and I are playing the camel,' said Cameron, rubbing his shaven head.

They were nearly over-balancing there and then. Jonathan wanted to be part of the act but he wasn't their size.

'That's great,' he said, but the boys weren't listening.

Reg had begun the song introduction. The children swayed first one way and then the other. Dimly, Jonathan remembered words about sheiks and private enterprise . . . Yes, the chorus was coming back to him.

'*Everything from socks to clocks*
Raspberry sundaes, frocks and undies . . .'

Jonathan didn't think their traders' goods were very suitable. Shouldn't they be selling cloves and garlic or something like incense? There ought to be some wise men around too to make the scene more serious. The song was tuneful, though. Jonathan found himself singing loudly and was pleased to hear that Cameron and Zak were well off key.

Bill stamped hard into the floor with his left boot. 'Please!' he shouted. 'This is a melody you should be able to follow clearly. Listen to Reg.'

Reg emphasised the notes in a slower tempo. Jonathan could hear the twang of the foot pedal as he played. He had a lot of feeling.

There was a break after the second round of the song. Amy had edged closer to Jonathan. For once, she wasn't looking down but directly at him, in a way that made her different. She no longer seemed so shy. Jonathan noticed how her eyes were violet in colour. Contrary to what he had always thought, she might not be such a boring person after all.

'I can be your wife if you like,' Amy said.

'What do you mean?' Jonathan was flattered.

'Some of the traders can have wives,' she explained. 'Bill said so.'

Amy linked arms with Jonathan and drew him into a stroll. 'We can talk about anything,' she went on.

'What are we selling?' Jonathan asked.

They continued to walk round in a circle as Amy thought very hard. 'Biological detergents,' she said.

They had nearly reached the piano. Then Jonathan had an inspiration. 'Coconut oil for cooking and for sunburn,' he said. 'My mum uses coconut oil on the beach in summer.'

Amy wasn't the type to argue. 'If you think so,' she replied.

The rehearsal room had taken on a warmth that went beyond artificial lighting. Bags and odd pieces of clothing were laid up against the walls in untidy heaps and the bar had been cleaned up. There was now a sense of familiarity and belonging.

Jonathan tried to imagine how the market scene would happen on stage. They were situated in the city of Pepperan in the land of the Blue Lotus. A very exotic-sounding place.

Walking with Amy, Jonathan felt that he was already in the tropics. He wanted to take his shirt off. He hoped she hadn't seen that he was sweating.

Chapter Eleven

Mia was given the role of the Peri, a magic fairy of the sea. She would be the guide to Sinbad and Prince Hassan in their search for the diamond Moor-El-Din.

While the other kids took a break, Mia and Bill stood together in discussion over her entrances and exits. Mia was plotting again. She had known instinctively that she would be chosen for Peri and had confided that much to her mother.

Jonathan, with his feet propped up against a tote bag, looked at them with mounting dismay. His drives with the Nathans would be even more awful from now on.

'Have some lemonade,' Amy said to him.

She had sat down in a heap beside him. Not far off

from them were the Parkview boys. Tom was rubbing his head with a towel.

'I don't want to dance anywhere near that Mia,' he said. 'Man, she's got attitude problems.'

Jonathan let Amy's lemonade trickle down his throat and revive him. He remembered Mia's smile when he had got out into the road to replace Mrs Nathan's lost cones.

Without any warning, Reg banged the lid down on his piano and left the room suddenly. He had a habit of doing that. Jonathan decided he was on the moody side, but then you had to make allowances for musicians. Mum and Dad would find his own temperament difficult as the opening loomed closer. The cast were very far from being ready. Tom was yawning. Zak had opened a packet of biscuits and threw a couple over to him. Zak's face was red from so much exertion, his freckles were livid now on his cheeks.

Tom caught the biscuits in one hand and they crumbled. 'Yo,' he said.

When Mia told her mother about the Peri part, Mrs Nathan got emotional for the second time that day.

'Oh, darling,' she gasped.

Then she said it again and Jonathan, who was following them out to the car, wanted to tell her to save her emotions for something proper, like a death. But he didn't. Mia balanced up ahead of him in a controlled *arabesque*. Jonathan had trouble holding on to his rucksack. He still had two hours of maths before the day was finished and tomorrow was scheduled for school.

Back at home, Jonathan practised his swaying routine in the bedroom mirror. The trouble was that if he moved too much one way, he went out of view. He made each sway smaller and inclined his body towards the floor until he ached all over. Jonathan still needed to hold his tummy in more and his fringe was too long. He would have to make a hairdresser's appointment.

Alex arrived unannounced after supper while Jonathan lay flat out on his bed. He was struggling with Test Three in his maths book, a repeat of yet another exercise for Hugs Bugs, whom he was due to see the following afternoon.

'The class think you're skiving,' Alex said to Jonathan by way of a greeting.

He didn't settle down but wandered the room, ill at ease in the confined space. Without possession of a ball, Alex became clumsy. He wore new trainers that had been bought with the idea of lasting. They made his feet look huge.

Jonathan didn't bother to answer the charge. His school was really pathetic.

'Which of these shapes is symmetrical?' he asked.

He was desperate, though he couldn't show it. Alex studied several possibilities.

'Option C, the third one,' he announced after a pause.

Jonathan thumped his bedspread and then the maths book itself, leaving a dented page. 'That's stupid,' he said.

Alex had lost interest. He had other things on his mind. 'My dad's back,' he said. 'He and mum are trying to work things out.'

Jonathan ticked option E for his answer in bold pencil.

Alex sat down beside him on the bed. 'Mum says she's broken three cups and four dinner plates since last Friday.'

Jonathan considered this. 'You can always eat with us,' he said, 'except we don't have a lot of food now that Mum's out so much. I've had spaghetti with tomato sauce two nights running and I don't even like spaghetti. It's not good for my weight.'

Jonathan had started to look at himself anxiously in the mirror again. Try as he might he couldn't even feel his cheekbones.

Alex threw a cushion at the glass. Then he took Jonathan's head into an arm lock until he yelped. Both boys keeled over and came up fighting. But they were laughing now and happy to be together.

'You'd better say hello to my dad,' Jonathan said, thinking that Alex might put him in a better mood. Since rehearsals had begun, conversation between them had sunk to a new low. Occasionally Jonathan caught his father's troubled gaze on him and he felt guilty without knowing why. Things were changing for the worse. What, he wondered, was he to do?

Jonathan and Alex could see the illuminated hut through the darkness, a shining beacon in an otherwise murky exterior. Houses beyond the Morrison home were screened by high laurel hedging to the sides and a flint wall at the bottom that concealed all but roof levels.

Usually Mr Morrison sat at his bench and trestle table, silhouetted against the windows. So absorbed would he be in his latest canvas that Jonathan was often able to slip in beside his father and surprise him.

But something was wrong. As the boys came closer, Jonathan instinctively knew that he wouldn't be there. His movements were always visible from some way off, even from the shadows that his crouching figure cast on the walls. Neither was there any tell-tale smoke escaping from the roof vent.

He hesitated.

'What's happening?' Alex asked from behind him.

The garden was still, as though any sign of wind had passed long before. In the distance, a train rattled through the night and left an echo.

Jonathan pushed the door open. A bottle of white spirit lay on the table and there was a smell of mouldy fruit hanging in the air. His father's latest painting stood on its easel in the corner of the hut. Jonathan's heart began to beat fast. A stroke of navy paint had been brushed across the canvas and all but cancelled the picture of a vase and two oranges.

'Wow,' said Alex. 'That's really cool presentation.' He folded his arms like a serious critic. 'I guess you'd call it Futurism.'

'Shut up,' Jonathan said quietly. He wanted to reach out to a hand that was not there. 'It's my turn,' he whispered now. 'Dad's gone.'

He was suddenly cold. The wood-burning stove had gone dead hours before and there were no familiar shadows on the walls. Only a lamp gave off shafts of uncertain light. This felt like a nothing place . . . Jonathan didn't need to look anywhere now. His father's departure had been sudden and perhaps unplanned.

'He'll come back,' Alex said. 'Mine did. They miss home cooking.'

Jonathan reflected on this and shook his head. 'Not in this house,' he said.

That day's newspaper had been flung wide open into a corner. It was not like his father to leave his paper unfolded after use. Almost idly, Jonathan took the pages up and saw the obituaries heading.

A picture in the bottom right corner held his attention. Just a face, very white and fragile, with luminous eyes that seemed to pierce him. They were the saddest eyes Jonathan had ever seen. The lines underneath read:

Dancer of dramatic intensity

Michelle Kavinska, who has died aged 77, was spotted by Nicholos Petrov in a 1956 production of Giselle in the Paris Opera.

She joined his company to take Russian classics to the New World. During an infamous train journey on the Pacific coast of America, Scheherazade's costumes and scenery caught fire in a tunnel. Everything was burnt. The company's subsequent performance took place notwithstanding.

There were hints of a liaison with Petrov's brother but this was never confirmed. Kavinska left the company five years later in London to marry anonymously. She returned to the stage as a cabaret entertainer, bringing her exotic continental style with her.

Michelle Kavinska

Dancer and cabaret artist

Born January 3, 1937, died November 5, 2014

His mother was calling them from the house.

Jonathan wanted to save the obituary without knowing why. Had his father been somehow affected in the same way? He would hold on to it until he came back. Perhaps his dad knew something about the woman.

Alex was already on his way inside. 'Let's get Barnaby,' he called out.

Jonathan had turned off the lamp in the hut. Now all contact with his father was at an even greater distance. He picked up a stone and threw it hard into the undergrowth.

Mrs Morrison was a small figure at the kitchen door. Jonathan wanted to shake her as though she were the cause of his father's misery, but instead he hugged her very tightly.

'Dad's gone,' he said.

Her hair needed combing and the marks each side of her mouth were deeper. 'I know, love,' she answered. 'Your father's not very well at the moment.'

'What's wrong with him?' asked Alex.

Mrs Morrison put an arm around each of their shoulders. 'He's depressed because he doesn't have a job and . . .' she hesitated. 'He doesn't like me working.'

Barnaby had escaped down to the floor where he shifted before scuttling around in circles.

'Or me,' said Jonathan. 'Is he coming back soon?' he asked.

The kitchen was very tidy. Every pot and pan from the last few days had been washed up and put away. His mother was busy again with arms in the sink and had her back to him.

'I don't know,' she said. Her voice was muffled.

Jonathan didn't want to ask any more questions. He would be getting his first pay packet on Friday and while Dad wasn't there, they would have to use his money. Jonathan could show his parents that he was responsible. He felt for the newspaper page that he had torn out and put it into his pocket. He wanted to read it again in the privacy of his room.

Jonathan wondered if Nureyev had had family problems. It was very difficult being the performer son of a mum and dad who argued all the time. Then he remembered that life had been difficult for Nureyev too. After all, he had been brought up under the Communists and forced to run away from Russia for ever.

Jonathan wasn't going to be able to run away because he was in a pantomime. He would have to stay at home and look after Mum and just hope that Dad would come back soon.

Chapter Twelve

The beginning of December brought snow and a nationwide freeze. Most travellers went skidding to their destinations. From the Morrison house, all routes seemed to lead uphill. Roads approaching the motorway had shrunk with their accumulated whiteness so that hedgerows lifted into tall cliffs and traffic drove by with no room for overtaking.

First thing in the mornings, Jonathan spent a lot of time with his mother trying not to get asphyxiated. Sitting in the garage and watching his mum pull on the choke was not his idea of fun. They needed a new car. So did Mrs Nathan. There were long delays and on at least two occasions Jonathan had needed to push-start Mrs

Nathan, only to then be left sprawled flat out in the road. This was annoying. He couldn't afford an injury so close to the show's opening in a week's time.

At school, Jonathan had taken to keeping the *Sinbad* script just inside his desk so that during the odd break he could continue to learn lines. Anything was possible during English and geography, but not this afternoon. At two-thirty p.m., Hugs Bugs was due to introduce them to a whole hour of algebra.

The kids had opened a window wide and someone was throwing snowballs into the classroom. Jason's woollen cap had been pulled off his head. Now he stomped up and down between the tables, clenching his fists for a rematch. There would be war later. Sam and Marcus were squabbling over a box of chocolates. Hugs Bugs never noticed that they usually ate through class.

Jonathan sighed. None of them understood that having a double life took a lot of staying power.

When Mrs Humphries came in, she brought pools of water with her that ran in rivulets from her calf-length boots. Her voice was failing again. Jonathan recognised the same hacking quality as his mother's exhaust.

'Settle down,' she said between coughs.

Hugs Bugs was laden with files that preceded her. A

pen and her class register had already fallen from the top of the pile.

'What a dipstick,' said Jason, but without malice.

There was a rustle of paper from Sam's box of chocolates. Outside, the snow continued to fall and nestle down along window ledges.

As Class 7 opened books, a muffled ringing came from the depths of Sam's drawer. It was his mobile, which he kept on everywhere he went. His mother usually rang him about this time and although Sam had suffered three detention periods for his sins, the class had come to expect her weather reports from New York.

They were waiting now.

'Yeah,' Sam said, clamping his mobile to his ear.

Mrs Humphries had finally found her seat. Now she tapped her pen impatiently.

Sam could suss what kind of mood Hugs Bugs was in. 'Got to go, Mum,' he said.

'How many times, Samuel, have you been told to switch off your mobile in class? Give it to me, please.' She had been through these confrontations before.

Sam was wriggling in his seat now. He switched his phone off. 'I'm sorry, Mrs Humphries,' he said. He couldn't contain himself. 'It's twenty-eight degrees below on 970 Fifth Avenue at ten-thirty a.m.,' he announced.

There was a general murmur of approval from the class.

Sam thought hard in order to get himself out of trouble. 'My mum's on a new type of Prozac,' he said. 'They're those pills that make you happy. I took one once.' He fingered the surface of his desk almost lovingly.

Mrs Humphries had resumed a more upright position. She was wheezing harder than she had the entire winter.

'If it's twenty-eight degrees below on 970 Fifth Avenue at ten-thirty a.m.,' she said, 'and the temperature is dropping one and a half degrees every three hours, what will it be at three-fifteen a.m. tomorrow morning?'

The class gave a groan.

A choir was singing 'Good King Wenceslas' on the floor above and Jonathan felt a surge of excitement at the prospect of Christmas. School would be closing soon. He peered outside at the empty playground surrounded by wire. The sky was a leaden grey.

Jonathan wondered how his dad was and where he might be staying.

With a bit of luck, he would be missing Mum.

On their first visit to the Albany Theatre, the children

were led straight to the stalls and told to keep quiet. Miss Spencer was rehearsing the soloist from the Moncrieff Ballet. There was no Reg to accompany her and in place of him the sound of violins came from a CD player.

The dancer was tiny, even smaller than Miss Spencer. She wore leg warmers over tights and a crochet top, rolling constantly through her feet to rise *en pointe*. Jonathan hoped that nobody would bump into her because she would just be bowled over.

'I can do that,' Mia said, her mouth a sullen line of disapproval. Already she was unhappy at the prospect of a rival.

The ballerina hung in there on one leg and a low *plié*, poised for some dramatic gesture as yet unknown to the audience.

The viewing was a luxury. Jonathan sat back in his plush velvet seat in the stalls and watched every movement. Perspectives here were quite different compared to The Cellars. Being so close to each other in that other place had made their work mechanical. The figures on stage created a distance that allowed the imagination to wander. Jonathan liked this. He wanted to be up there too, as a protective nobleman and chief escort to the Moncrieff ballerina.

Miss Spencer seemed to have found her energy again as she coaxed the dancer to the wings with a frenzy of outstretched arms. The younger woman sprang after her and they disappeared from sight.

'That's Princess Pearl's cry for freedom,' said Mia to whoever was listening. 'She wants to choose her own suitor so that she isn't forced into marriage by her father.'

Mia was propped against her closed seat, which gave her a better view. She swung it down and up with a series of repetitious bangs.

Miss Spencer had returned to the stage. More imperious with her new height, she faced out into the auditorium. 'Sit still, Mia,' she ordered.

Mia came down with another bang.

'You are professionals and I expect you to behave that way.'

Mia let her seat swing up with a bigger bang. 'Bossy boots!' she hissed.

Once on stage, the kids ran about unsteadily, surprised at how the floor sloped down towards the orchestra pit. Jonathan found the view from where he stood alarming. There were tiers of seats above him: a circle, a dress circle and what Bill had earlier called 'the gods'. This was where students without much money could see the show.

Jonathan would have to remember to look up at them too. Right now, though, he had a problem walking in a straight line.

At last the boys had a number to learn without the girls. The sailors would board the ship to the beat of a modern number. As Miss Spencer showed them the initial choreography, Jonathan's heart began pounding. He understood jazz and stuff. Hadn't he done it all before in the Neptune's production of Michael Jackson's 'Thriller'? Tom and the others were totally ballet trained. Jonathan would be able to show them what he knew, which was a lot.

Miss Spencer placed the four boys diagonally and took them through the sequence. 'Behind, side, step, kick, circle . . . wiggle, wiggle, hip . . . in, out, step, click. Repeat.'

Tom was going ahead of Jonathan and finding the razor-sharp head and clipped body actions easy. The other boys, Zak and Cameron, were slower on the pick up. Jonathan thought he was probably somewhere in-between. He would have overtaken Tom but he had to stay in the right order, which felt annoying.

'You're too far forward, Tom,' called Miss Spencer. 'Get back!'

They were turning now to face the left.

'That's better, boys, but you're going off stage, Jonathan. Move back into line ...'

Bill had come to join Miss Spencer. He surveyed the group thoughtfully. 'Not bad,' he said. 'But Tom is definitely the pick of the bunch.'

Miss Spencer shook her head. 'Tom is all technique. Look at Jonathan. He is developing a real 'presence', along with that elevation. The talent is there, mark my words.'

Bill could only see that the boy was puffing badly. 'He's not got what it takes,' he muttered.

He didn't add that, to his mind, Jonathan was immature compared to the Parkview students. The standard and sophistication of those boys stood out a mile.

Bill had a lot to think about. Reg was sulking in the bar and the stage manager had problems with the boat. On top of everything else, he was trying to persuade Sinbad down from Norwich. The actor was already overdue.

The music had come to an end.

Tom hunched over his knees, panting hard. 'I got it, man,' he announced.

He gave Jonathan a brisk shove. 'Just follow me,' he said. 'I'm gonna show you the way.'

Tom was half turning again to face the auditorium where the other kids waited for their call.

Jonathan's competitive edge was on the wane. He had to admit that even apart from those cheekbones, Tom was cool. The boys were grouped casually and chatting between themselves. Up there on a real stage for the first time in his life, Jonathan felt a teeny bit lonely.

Doors were banging loudly from an outside passage. Bill had moved from his discussion, and all that could be heard now were strange mutterings from the back. These grew in volume.

The voice was that of one man's and as he came towards the stage, those watching him were aware of some mighty presence. He had a deep and majestic voice, capable of Shakespearian wrath.

'This is a godforsaken place,' the man said. 'Is anybody at home?!'

Chapter Thirteen

The man continued to walk through the aisle between children who sat both sides of him. He was very large and leant heavily on a stick, one foot trailing behind the other. At first he kept his head low. Then, as he reached the orchestra pit, the man shaded his eyes to avoid the glare from the lights and waved his stick at those above him.

'Come aboard, sir,' said Bill with a wry grin.

This was the arrival he had been waiting for and a man of such stature had the right to bide his time. After another couple of minutes, the figure clambered painfully onto the stage.

'I've been in more celebrated places,' he said, ' and I wouldn't like a repetition of my train journey. No restaurant car . . . not even a waiter . . .'

The man drew his walking stick close to his ample stomach. He had thick, jet black hair that was brushed in a wave across his forehead. It contrasted strangely with his well-lived-in face, full of enough lines to mark a road map. He was not a young man. His smile, which was only occasional, showed perfect teeth. He wore a full-length raincoat and suede shoes that bore all the evidence of his journey.

'We're into the Dark Ages,' he announced.

His eyes were quick as he appraised the other people present. They were luminous eyes of no particular colour . . . perhaps grey or green . . . you couldn't tell. The kids still looked at him, intent on the new arrival.

Bill introduced Miss Spencer and she shook hands with him formally.

'A dancer, I do believe,' the man said with grace.

Miss Spencer laughed.

'Our choreographer for the duration,' said Bill, 'and she is performing miracles with this bunch, I can assure you.'

For just a moment, Miss Spencer appeared to be blushing.

'Who is he?' whispered Tom. He too was in awe of this man.

'I think it's the Caliph,' replied Cameron, 'but I'm not sure.'

Jonathan was aware of a general disappointment. He for one had always imagined the Caliph as swarthy and athletic with a goatee beard. He didn't think this guy and his walking stick held much promise.

'A touch of gout,' the man was explaining to Bill. He tried to bend his bad knee and winced. 'Won't last,' he said, 'but the pain is terrible. Doctor says I've got to cut down on my Special Brew.'

The man walked a few steps in a circle just to show Bill that he remained mobile.

'Rehearsal tomorrow morning at ten o'clock sharp for you, Hassan and the Wazir,' said Bill. 'Sorry it's an early call.' He looked at his watch and swore under his breath. 'We're done for today, everyone,' he added. 'Out of time, yet again.'

Miss Spencer was removed from the gathering and half hidden in some gauze curtains. She had held up well during rehearsal. Now once again the sweating had come upon her, as if she were in the grip of fever. The fabric she touched shook as she drew its folds about her. Unseen, Miss Spencer took a couple of pills from a small bottle she kept in the pocket of her cardigan and swallowed them fast. She found a tap at the bottom of some stairs and, cupping her hands, let the water run into them. Miss Spencer couldn't drink fast enough.

The Moncrieff ballet dancer had wandered onto the stage. She marked out a series of *pas de basques*, which led into a slow practice waltz without her partner. The actions were almost careless.

Miss Spencer was back. No, not like that, she mused. She would correct the girl when she had the strength and advise her on more lyrical arm work. Tomorrow, perhaps. Miss Spencer knew she must get home . . . make an appointment with her doctor for the test results she had delayed for too long.

'You don't look well.' Bill was beside her as she came out into the open.

'I'm fine,' Miss Spencer said. 'Just a bit tired.'

She wished that Bill's turquoise and yellow shirt was less glaring. He had always been an unusual dresser, even in the old days.

'I like what you're doing with the kids,' Bill told her. 'They're coming along fine.'

'I think so,' Miss Spencer said softly.

They walked arm in arm through the paraphernalia of wire and cable backstage. She was light-headed, and remembering thirty-second changes in the wings. Many seasons ago, the roar of final applause had so often been hers.

A stagehand was addressing Bill. 'The boat's ready,' he said. He had thickset arms and a broad chest.

'Good,' Bill said. 'Put it in the scene dock.'

Bill guided Miss Spencer around planks of wood blocking their path. 'Something's going right,' he said wearily. 'Let's hope that Sinbad will decide to join his boat shortly.'

Mia was behind the two of them. 'Excuse me, Bill,' she said. She came forward with a friendly smile.

Miss Spencer began to walk through the stalls.

'Well,' said Bill. 'What can I do for you, Mia?'

She was coy, as the moment demanded. 'I wanted to let you know that my mum can help with the costumes,' she said. 'She makes all of mine. She's very good, my mum.'

Bill Jones hesitated. 'I'm sure she is,' he answered, 'but we have a wardrobe mistress and an assistant.'

Mia frowned. She hadn't bargained for rejection. Her mum was already drawing up patterns and would be bound to take offence.

'You just concentrate on your Peri role,' Bill said. 'That's what I want.'

The girl let out a loud sigh. She was about to argue, but Miss Spencer was calling her from the top of the auditorium.

'Go and get changed immediately, Mia. You're late.'

Mia turned again to Bill. 'I was wondering about my costume . . .' she mused. 'My mum thinks . . .'

Bill was walking away. 'Run along and join the others,' he said without a backward glance.

The changing rooms were cramped and smelt of paint. The boys were in room five, with a counter that ran the same length as the mirror fixtures. A collection of slanting sixty-watt bulbs gave off surprising heat. Jonathan decided that he would feel more at home in these surroundings when he was dressed and fully made-up for the occasion.

Tom had bagged a position closest to the door. Now he sat defining what was good about his face in the glass.

'I'm so hot,' said Zak. 'I need a break.'

He sat slumped in a swivel chair. His freckles had given him extra red cheeks and he swung his legs up to rest across the counter.

Tom moved a few paces to the right. 'This place is foul,' he announced. 'Much smaller than our last changing room.'

Tom swung back on his heels and gave a hip roll, which lifted his heels. He twisted and did the same thing again. 'We're in this together . . .' he sang in a falsetto voice.

He pointed directly at Jonathan. 'Even you, sunshine,' he said.

The three Parkview boys laughed.

'Let's go swimming early tomorrow. It might be good for our muscles,' said Cameron. 'I'm aching all over.'

The other boys cheered. 'Yo,' they said in unison.

'You too,' said Tom, gesturing towards Jonathan. 'Your diaphragm's pathetic.' He flexed his biceps to show his authority.

'You wanna come?' asked Zak.

Jonathan continued to pack his dance gear into his tote bag. The boys exchanged glances. Jonathan didn't like swimming. He had private study the next day and there was no getting out of it. More maths . . . followed by another rehearsal late afternoon.

This time tomorrow, Jonathan thought suddenly, he might be dead.

'OK,' he said.

Tom tapped the side of the counter. 'We'll swim before breakfast,' he said. 'Nine a.m. because there's no school.'

Not for you, thought Jonathan with a heavy heart.

'Yo,' replied Zak. 'We can have breakfast afterwards.'

The boys had left long before Mrs Morrison arrived to pick Jonathan and Mia up at the stage door.

'Sorry . . .' she said and was about to explain herself, but there was no point.

Even Mia had gone quiet. The kids were both too tired to argue.

Jonathan sat between a crate of mineral water and some packets of grain for Barnaby. He was squashed, as usual, but had let Mia go in front with his mother for a bit of peace and quiet.

The snow was a camouflage of white that made every shape mysterious. Overhead, as they drove through the centre of town, banners illuminated with the three wise men swung high above them.

Jonathan bent forward and buried his head in his mother's left shoulder. 'Any news?' he whispered, not wanting Mia to hear him.

His mother gave him a nudge with her elbow. 'No, love,' she said and Jonathan moved back again.

'Look!' exclaimed Mia. She was pointing towards the square ahead and leaning across Mrs Morrison. 'The

Christmas tree has lost a big branch. It's all lopsided,' she said.

Mrs Morrison glanced briefly in the same direction. 'What a shame,' she said.

Sure enough, there was a branch missing. The tree had lost its festive air.

For a moment the giant fir seemed to cry out to Jonathan, as though they shared the loss of a limb. That was what it was like losing Dad, he thought – a sudden amputation that neither of them were ready for.

Chapter Fourteen

The water in the pool was pale green in colour and gave off shimmering reflections. Bathers swam up and down their selected lengths, some cautious and others more intent on a training regime. One or two spectators sat above them. At eight-fifteen a.m., the place was already full.

Jonathan stood halfway down the side of the baths, shivering. He wore bathing trunks that had fitted him once but now pinched into his waist. The Parkview boys were no strangers to the water. Tom had made a perfect dive, having poised for a split second beforehand like an Olympic contender, and rose again with hardly a ripple. Cameron and Zak were noisy, rather than accomplished, swimmers. They crawled together intermittently and then rested against the bar at the deep end.

'You're just sad, Jonathan!' shouted Cameron.

He was pinching his nose and balancing off the rail. Jonathan pretended not to hear. He was going to join them very soon but not until he felt ready. He watched the troop of toddlers siphoned off in a shallow playing area, and envied them their arm-bands. It was make or break time.

Jonathan sighed. He rose up on his toes as Tom had done and put his arms out directly in front of him. Then he breathed deeply. But his grip was slipping. Jonathan went forward with a crash and met the water horizontally. It was the belly flop of the century.

Pain gripped his whole body and made his head pound. He was stuck near the bottom of the pool, and the rage that went through him was as bad as the physical trauma.

'Your stomach is bright red,' Tom said to Jonathan as they towelled down afterwards. 'You must have hit the water very hard.' He was whistling and fiddling with his wet hair, which rose in spikes.

'No, I didn't,' lied Jonathan. If he bent down gently in a minute, he would just be able to put his trainers on.

The Parkview boys ate bacon, egg, sausage and tomato in the canteen upstairs. They drank fresh orange drinks.

Jonathan wasn't hungry. He couldn't even manage his toast. Zak got up and played with the slot machines until a lot of tokens came out.

Jonathan definitely wasn't going to go swimming again. It was stupid to have allowed the boys to persuade him. He didn't want to take any more risks because he might end up covered in bandages.

Nureyev wouldn't have gone to his local pool so near to an engagement. Jonathan had a hunch that he would have considered swimming beneath him. After all, Nureyev had done really dangerous things like leaping through an open window for *La Spectre de la Rose*. Now that was wicked.

Jonathan got his break later in the day. Hugs Bugs had caught a real cold and his maths session was off.

Mrs Morrison took the phone call. 'You've got a reprieve,' she said, but could only think that Peter would not have been happy with the news.

'Whoopee!' Jonathan cried.

He picked up a plate and did a little samba in the kitchen. That was what his father would have called it, anyway.

His mother was at home more often now, having given

up her extra hours at the garden centre. She went quiet sometimes, which was a sign of how much she missed Dad. Jonathan didn't think there was any contest. He knew that he missed him more.

Mrs Morrison was cooking real food again and after Jonathan had eaten two helpings of lasagne, he felt a lot better.

'Mum, I want you to look at something,' he said.

He produced the grimy obituaries page from his pocket and laid it flat on the table.

'What, love?' Mrs Morrison was concentrating as she scoured the sink and made everything around her clean. There had to be method now . . . nothing left undone.

She had cancelled her meetings with new suppliers for the next week. That would give her some time, but no extra cash, which was badly needed. Mrs Morrison didn't want to be far away from home in case he came back.

'Mum!'

She looked directly at her one and only child. Jonathan had gelled his hair in a half roll. His eyes met hers without sign of the usual rebellion. The strain was there for both of them.

'I found this in the hut,' Jonathan said.

The black-and-white photograph was creased now and Mrs Morrison had to read the small print closely. 'So . . .' she said. She didn't know what he was on about.

Jonathan tried to explain. 'Dad never leaves his newspapers unfolded. The paper was thrown on the floor and it was open on this page. Maybe he knew the dancer who died.'

He hesitated, uncertain, but wanting to unravel anything that had led to his father's departure.

'Darling, with so much on his mind, he probably missed the obituaries altogether.'

Mrs Morrison read the paragraph again and then glanced at the photo. The woman did remind her of somebody but she couldn't think who. She thought back . . . and checked herself . . . Yes, she had seen that face before . . .

'Well, she certainly led an exotic life,' Mrs Morrison said carefully. She didn't want to talk about this mystery figure any further.

'But did you know her?' Jonathan blurted out.

Mrs Morrison had begun to unload damp clothes from the washing basket. She took a pair of jeans and stretched them hard, laying them out finally across the ironing board.

'Did you know her or not?' shouted Jonathan. The red flush was beginning at the base of his neck.

'No, of course not,' Mrs Morrison said. 'And please don't raise your voice. I've got a headache.'

'My tummy hurts,' said Jonathan.

His mother's sympathy wasn't forthcoming. She continued to iron with harsh jabs at a jean leg and said nothing.

Her silence annoyed him so he went upstairs to his room. There Jonathan picked up his maths book and tried to work out from Section IV: Shapes and Space how many spots should be added to an unfinished line. He counted the first pattern and the second and then he was seeing spots. Hundreds of spots lined the edge of the page – balloons that flew about his bed.

Mrs Morrison went on ironing. She had an interview with the Income Support Agency later and would have to go through the whole story. She shuddered. That awful place where marital conflict was made public and then filed. She pressed the steam button and felt heat scald the underside of her chin. Mrs Morrison could see the outline of the hut through the kitchen window from where she stood – a ramshackle wooden building which now seemed remote as a place to be working in.

Alex rang Jonathan on his mobile, just as he was dozing off.

'Sam wants to make his birthday party a sleepover,' Alex said. 'He's organising everything.'

'What are you getting him?' asked Jonathan.

'We can't do better than his mum. She buys him all those expensive presents from New York.'

'We could take him to see that new vampire film,' said Alex.

'I haven't got time to go to the cinema,' replied Jonathan. His best friend just didn't understand the needs of a performer. And how could he ask for extra money right now?

'How's your mum?' Alex asked.

Jonathan stifled a yawn. The early swim had nearly done him in. 'Twitchy,' he said. 'One minute she's cross, the next minute she's sad.'

Alex was surprisingly tactful at times. 'Could be the weather,' he reflected.

Jonathan felt like spitting. 'It's Dad,' he said, 'and I've got to go for rehearsal now.'

His stomach remained tender. At least they would be

working to the script with lead actors and not dancing. Jonathan was pretty cool about his routine tonight.

Late that same evening, and long after her visit to the Income Support Agency, Mrs Morrison sat downstairs on her own and watched TV until she felt near to screaming. She then tried sewing a button onto one of Peter's shirts but the memories that she associated with it made her fingers shake.

Some whim drew her to his study, as if being there might give her contact with him.

Jonathan was right about his father's papers. There they were in orderly piles, with some on his desk and the remainder put away. Charmian opened the top file without reason. A jumble of words met her that made little sense. As she leafed through an EU personnel brochure, she saw that Peter had ringed various names. Beside each, he had drawn a caricature of a face, one with a nose just like Pinocchio's. At the bottom of one of the pages was an outline of a bull.

Mrs Morrison had no doubt left in her mind. Her husband had gone mad.

She made a decision and left the study, closing the door behind her. The stairs creaked as she went quietly on up, certain of what she must do. Jonathan's light was out. Mrs Morrison took the stepladder and lined it to the attic door, steadily climbing one rung at a time.

At the top of the house, every nocturnal creature seemed to haunt her in their call of the night. Cobwebs clung to rafters. On the floor were rolled-up dusty rugs and empty picture frames.

She knelt down and snapped open the trunk that held the many years of Morrison family history. This was forbidden territory but there was no stopping her now. Woollen scarves belonging to Peter's father were soft to the touch. There were Ordinance Survey maps, rusty trophies for county running, and a shiny sou'wester.

At the bottom of the trunk, Mrs Morrison found what she was looking for. The old family album binding her husband's northern roots had faded from its former glory. She turned the pages separated by tissue through a hazy progression of figures, then on to Peter as a baby, followed by the sullen teenager always in the company of his father. Fishing and climbing at Hardcastle Craggs . . . the two of them inseparable.

The image of the woman met her full force and she was not ready. Mrs Morrison took hold of the newspaper cutting she had kept since Jonathan's disclosure and compared the two photographs. Those dark haunting eyes held such sorrow. She felt for a moment as if she might faint. The faces were identical.

Chapter Fifteen

Reg sat on his stool at the end of the bar, having just drunk a neat vodka. He was feeling good. The staff at the Cock and Pheasant were unobtrusive and left him alone. They never worried the resident artists. Customers came and went but players at the Albany Theatre commanded special status. They spent their money freely after hours.

Reg had begun to merge the drone of conversation with the tinkling of a concerto in his head. Now he longed for Bill's arrival so that he could share this source of inspiration. Sometimes Reg could hear voices from Heaven.

'Another one, Reg?'

The Caliph and Sinbad had joined up at a nearby

table. They were old friends and stage partners. The script had been brought up to scratch by the two of them, an achievement to be proud of. The Caliph, however, was still in the wars and his leg hurt. He was also very sober, under the effects of lemonade.

'Get him a drink, for goodness' sake,' he said to Sinbad, 'his conducting is driving us all to the brink.'

Reg continued to sway on his stool. His voices were now in the crescendo.

'All right, all right,' grumbled Sinbad, fiddling for change. He had a long, lugubrious face that belied his athletic powers. They were geared to a profession in pantomime.

'Another lemonade?' he asked the Caliph.

The Caliph sighed. He saw no end to his sorry plight. 'Is there a drink with a bit more zip in it?' he sighed.

Bill Jones had just entered. 'A gin and tonic, please,' he called out as Sinbad made his way to the bar. Bill flung his technical notes on to the intervening table. 'The boat's finished,' he announced. 'We can rehearse the sailing scene now that everyone is here.' Bill looked doubtfully at the Caliph's leg. 'What about your costume fitting?' he asked.

The Caliph sighed again. 'It took me an hour to dress this morning,' he said.

Bill made a mental note to remind the wardrobe mistress that the Caliph had put on about three kilos since their last meeting. Then his eye caught sight of Reg leaning almost horizontally to the bar. 'What's he doing?' he muttered.

'Overtaking Bach,' replied the Caliph. 'He's on his seventh vodka, the old devil.'

Bill had a strong desire to shake Reg. He was supposed to be working on the show, not his own internal compositions. 'Cheers,' he murmured instead as he took a large swallow of gin.

Sinbad was turning the pages of his script with interest. 'I like the alterations,' he said. 'But you might have told me that you were cutting some of my most important lines.'

'Not just yours,' answered Bill, 'the whole piece needs tightening up or the audience will start snoring.'

Sinbad stood up and slammed his glass down on a table. 'Nobody has ever gone to sleep during my performance,' he said between clenched teeth.

As he spoke, Reg began conducting the air with his arms. 'Boom, ba ba, boom,' he sang to the crowded room.

The Caliph winked slyly at Sinbad. 'Oh dear, oh dear, oh dear,' he said.

Reg was now singing loudly. 'Tra, di di da aaa . . . di di dum . . . tra la . . .'

He tried to wave in Bill's direction, but Bill was no longer there. The singing faded until Reg stared ahead of him without a peep.

'Let's hope his inspiration will carry through to our show,' remarked the Caliph.

Sinbad went on looking at his script. 'Yeah,' he said, 'otherwise a lot of us will be up the creek.'

There was plenty of activity on stage. While various technicians tested wiring and lights, Tom was being lifted into the wings by a hoist. The children watched as he went higher and higher and began to move across.

'All right, Tom?' Miss Spencer called up to him, in charge of this operation.

'I'm coming,' the boy replied and his words were distant, from so far away. Then he glided over to the other side, graceful as an animal in the wild, and the kids were disbelieving that Tom could reach such a great height.

'And again,' shouted Miss Spencer, 'but let your legs hang looser.'

Tom let his legs relax. After all, he had the hook to hold him. From where he was the rest of the cast were small fry.

'Wow!' squealed Mia. 'Isn't he amazing?' She hopped on one foot with excitement.

Jonathan said nothing. For him, this was yet another occasion where Tom had proved his ability. Mia pushed Jonathan out of her path without noticing. As if to emphasise a secret bond, she twisted the friendship bracelet around on her left wrist.

'I'm free!' sang Tom.

He was now being released slowly to the ground. The children gathered round him.

'What's it like?' asked Cameron.

'It's brilliant,' puffed Tom as a man unhooked him from behind. Tom had no qualms about being up there at a height that was rightfully his.

Miss Spencer was beckoning to Jonathan. 'Your turn,' she said and she was smiling.

'Me?' Jonathan felt hot and cold in turn, thinking that Miss Spencer had made a mistake.

'Not him,' said Zak.

The other kids too were shifting unhappily with her choice.

'Jonathan is Tom's understudy for his two solos,' she said firmly. 'Both you and Cameron have costume changes.'

Tom was tapping the side of his head as if to suggest

that Miss Spencer was insane.

'Off you go, the lot of you,' she said. 'Drinks break for twenty minutes.'

'That's not fair!' burst out Zak. His freckles had risen like hives.

Tom put a careless arm around his shoulders. 'No worries,' he said as they walked away. 'That boy is bound to be scared of heights.'

Their laughter trickled off, and the other children followed them out of sight.

'Just relax into it,' advised Miss Spencer as the same man fitted Jonathan into the harness.

She then gave the thumbs up for the lift and Jonathan found himself quite weightless, rising to the top of the proscenium arch. From there, he saw the theatre in all its magnificence: the tiers that rose from the dress circle, and the small passageways higher still where people stood. Underneath him, he peered at the far-away figures of Miss Spencer and the others who, in turn, peered back at him.

Jonathan experienced a surge of power. For seconds, the audience were there, glued to their seats and cheering him on. He swung from the right, forming a *grand jeté* in the air and wanted to cry out loud.

'Keep your legs together,' called Miss Spencer from a long way off.

To Jonathan, her voice was a thin reed of sound.

As he descended, a hidden drum began to roll with a crashing of cymbals until he was deafened. The noise came from the pit.

Bill had returned and both he and Miss Spencer had fingers in their ears. Then a man's head appeared parallel with the stage.

'That's the drum solo,' the head announced. Reg identified himself further by putting on his glasses.

Bill had taken hold of the gold chain around his neck and was clenching it in frustration. 'Belt up!' he shouted.

Miss Spencer tried to placate him. 'Don't be cross with him,' she said. She was ready to stand between them if need be.

Jonathan was unhooked from his harness.

'Good work,' Miss Spencer whispered and then indicated that he should disappear. Jonathan thought Bill might burst with rage, but he didn't wait to witness a further scene.

As he came out into the wings, Amy was waiting for him.

'That was neat,' she said. 'You were really great.'

Jonathan tried to appear casual. 'Thanks,' he replied.

Amy was quite pretty really and, today, her eyes were the colour of violet.

'I came to get you,' she said.

'What for?' asked Jonathan.

'We've got a costume fitting and it's your turn,' Amy said.

As they went down into the basement and through a series of corridors, Jonathan realised that he had a friend. He didn't mind Amy as his trader's wife at all.

In fact, he had a sudden desire to stop in his tracks and take her hand.

'She's weird,' whispered Amy as she knocked on the door of room number nine.

He had no time to ask questions. Jonathan was inside before he knew it and without Amy. He stood alone.

There were conflicting smells here of musty silks and coffee. The room was full of costumes, wide skirts, brocaded waistcoats, odd hoops and material in every available space. On a high table sat an old sewing machine next to reels of cotton and the paraphernalia of a work basket.

The woman reminded him of a gypsy. She wore a full-length blue skirt and lace gloves cut off at the fingertips.

These revealed scarlet nails that scratched the surface of her table at regular intervals.

'So . . .' she said by way of a greeting, 'we hav de last boy . . .' The woman shuffled stiffly as she came towards Jonathan and he realised that she was no longer young.

'S-sorry I'm late,' he stammered.

'Tak off yor top,' she said, 'so I mezure you.'

Jonathan took off his top reluctantly. In the corner he had just noticed a mangy poodle lying on a blanket. The dog bared her teeth at Jonathan and growled.

'Shhh, Dottie,' the woman said. 'Behav yourself.'

She was pulling several shirts with flouncy sleeves off hangers and then a variety of baggy trousers that fastened at the ankle. The woman peered closely at Jonathan. A scarf hid most of her hair and was folded low so that it cut across her pencilled-in eyebrows.

'So . . .' she said again. 'You have ze stars in you.'

Jonathan struggled to pull on a shirt. 'I don't understand,' he said through the neckpiece. 'What do you mean?'

The woman opened her hands wide as if surprised. 'You have ze theatre already . . . You have ze ballet in yor family somewhere.'

Jonathan was unexpectedly angry. The costume he tried on smelt of mothballs.

'No I don't,' he answered. The shirt prickled his chest. 'That's just the trouble.'

The woman fastened buttons at his neck. 'You don no anythink,' she said. 'But I tell you, you ave ze stars on yor horizon.'

She measured different harem pants against him, clicking with annoyance. 'Try these ones,' she said finally and turned her back on Jonathan.

He was thankful she had lost interest. She gave him the heebie-jeebies.

The dog wasn't just growling now. She had left her cushion and was coming straight for him.

The woman spoke two words in a foreign language that he guessed was Russian. The dog slunk back with a whine.

'See!' she said to Jonathan.

She was watching him after all through the mirror. The harem pants flashed silver and ballooned over his calves. Jonathan decided that with a cutlass in his hand, he would be ready for any mortal combat.

Chapter Sixteen

The graveyard at Heptonstall was overgrown and hilly, a place for those wanting seclusion. Uneven flagstones gaped within metres of each other and the paths that ran between them led nowhere but into long grass.

Peter Morrison had trudged nearly two kilometres to get here. Above him stood the church, surrounded by fields as far as the eye could see. The caw of birds made shrill cries from an upper tract of land. Otherwise all was quiet.

The slab of marble on his father's grave had a new inscription that shocked him to the core.

Michelle Morrison

Dearest wife of Anthony Morrison

Born January 3, 1937

Died November 5, 2014

'In their separation they were never apart'

Mr Morrison read the words again and again and still he could not believe them. His mother who had abandoned him at the age of four was here beneath him and only just buried. He tried to understand why his father might have lied to him . . . to recall the childhood that he had long suppressed.

For a moment, Peter could again experience the stillness of the big house and the aching loneliness he had felt among a succession of carers as his father shut himself away behind doors.

Later came the bare facts, as he had learnt them. That his mother had disappeared with a dance troupe to the continent, leaving only a note. His father's grief. How Peter must never mention her name in his presence. How as the years went by he never did.

When he heard that she had died abroad, he was eighteen and without any sense of maternal attachment. Peter had won his university place at Durham and become passionate about sport, with a talent for sprinting. He had a new life.

It was after his father's death that Peter had begun to think about her again. During the last few months his mother had travelled in and out of his reveries like a random butterfly. Now he had no way of finding out the truth. He was too late.

There were fresh flowers at the head of his parents' grave. Peter wondered if anyone might have gone to her funeral service. Had she in her last moments remembered him?

'Peace at last.'

The voice came from nowhere. With a start, Peter turned to face an old woman in a black coat and hat who might have flown for the silence of her arrival. The woman had the air of town about her. She was an incongruous figure in this remote corner of Yorkshire.

'I'm s-sorry,' he stammered. Peter was afraid of this woman on the territory he now considered his own. He was only distantly aware that she might hold the key to the past and those lost lives.

'Michelle always loved him, you know. He was much too hard on her. In the end she couldn't take it . . .'

The woman looked at Peter but without curiosity. She

had the small form of a dancer, but had now gone brittle and stooped with age. The brim of her hat swooped down on one side, closing off a portion of her face. 'Who are you?' she asked.

'I'm a distant cousin,' said Peter quickly.

If he wasn't careful, he would become confessional. Yet there was no warmth in her to draw him out.

'Anthony hated the theatre. He was jealous of her friends and resented her work. He tried to stop Michelle performing altogether and for a while she did. But domesticity didn't suit her and she began taking the odd engagement. Anthony couldn't live with it. He was always criticising Michelle and, in the end, she went away for good.'

Peter tried hard to sound normal. 'What about her son?' he asked.

The woman hesitated. 'Michelle begged Anthony to allow her to visit him but he was adamant. He said she wasn't a proper mother and eventually there was no contact between them. When the rumours went about that she had died in a car crash in Monte Carlo, Anthony could come to terms with the loss.'

Peter wanted to shout out his identity, to stop the pain, which was in that instant a physical thing.

'He lived a lie,' the woman said. 'Later Anthony discovered that she had survived the crash, but to him she just didn't exist. No one could argue with him. I think Michelle gave up after that. The remaining household gradually fell apart and who knows what happened to the son. I don't think the two of them ever had contact again.'

The woman was stumbling on the stones as she turned towards the gate. 'Anthony tried to destroy Michelle's art,' she murmured. 'But he paid for it. The two of them had a great love. In the end, she couldn't live without her ballet.'

Peter wanted to ask this stranger more, to in some way delay her leaving. The woman was moving now across the path to the wooden gate that gave out onto woodland below. Who was she and where had she come from?

Her figure was losing its shape as she walked on and Peter had an urgent need to call her back. But when he tried to speak, the words froze in his mouth.

He had never felt so alone. The engraving that commemorated the union of his parents seemed to tilt as he read each letter again. Peter found himself crying and remembering all the years that had passed without his mother.

At the end of it all, he had no more emotion to give way to, only the certainty that the events leading to his family trauma must be put behind him. He couldn't bring either his mother or his father back.

As Peter stood there in the churchyard, a sensation of wind ruffled his clothes. But he was quite calm. Looking up, the skies had drawn in to form a canopy overhead, and on the hills visibility was fading. It was very cold. He knew without doubt that there would be snow before nightfall.

Jonathan saw the same sky much later from his bedroom window. Frost below the sash was already splintering and a lone, glimmering star pierced the night. When he put his face to the glass, ice stung his cheek.

He was an hour late for Sam's birthday party and this time he couldn't blame his mother. Jonathan had problems deciding what to wear because all his best clothes needed ironing. Finally he chose his frayed jeans and a sweatshirt, which were at the bottom of the pile. They were still damp.

Jonathan went downstairs and was glad of the creaks underneath the stair carpet. The house felt too quiet. The guinea pig had taken to burying himself in Jonathan's right slipper and lay there now. He was in a nipping mood.

'I think Barnaby's worried,' Jonathan said to his mum.

Mrs Morrison stroked the fur between the guinea pig's ears. 'Animals pick up on our feelings, you know.'

They were both silent. Jonathan was aware again of how every pot and pan was in its place. His mum had been putting things away.

'When is he coming back?' he asked, not for the first time. The sensation of his heart beating was unexpectedly loud.

'I don't know,' Mrs Morrison said. 'But he will, love, I know he will.'

Jonathan saw his mother's face tighten, the way her hair hung loosely without curl. He knew then that she wasn't certain about anything.

'It's snowing,' he said.

Wherever his dad was tonight, he could only hope he would be keeping warm.

'D'you want me to stay with you?' Jonathan asked.

'Don't be silly,' his mother said. 'Sam and the others would never forgive me. Have you got your pyjamas?'

Jonathan was pleased he was going overnight but felt guilty at the same time. As the only son, he should be looking after her.

The snow had gathered at the windows, lining in drifts

to create a white cloud. Jonathan felt Barnaby quiver in his hands.

'Here, Mum,' he said. He gave the guinea pig over and picked up his bag.

A series of quick hoots came from a car outside, quite different to those of Mrs Nathan's. Her hoots were always wailing.

'Alex's dad,' Jonathan said. He still stood on the same spot.

'Off you go,' his mother said, 'and be good. I'll see you in the morning.'

When Jonathan opened the front door, he gasped.

Everything was white and the cold air enveloped him. His footprints as he went to join Alex were like those of a giant in the snow.

Chapter Seventeen

Sam's father had only appeared once and that was to steal a bag of Kettle Chips. He was now upstairs, having promised to keep out of the way. This was a party for kids only.

Sam's birthdays were an annual event. The entire Year Seven had come over last year, but this time around invitations were more selective. When Jonathan and Alex arrived, there were just nine friends in the living room.

Jason had taken up all the sofa, which stretched from one wall to the other. His baseball cap was tilted forward, giving the impression of broody concentration. The sofa was covered by a sheet. Sam's mother had allergies to dust and animals and even though she resided permanently in

New York, her husband hadn't yet got round to changing the decoration.

Next to the abstract picture of swirling brush strokes was an orange lava lamp that had been recycled, another import from the US.

'What are those flickering bits moving about in the light?' Jonathan asked Alex. The whole place had made his heartbeat start up again.

'Amoebas,' said Alex with complete certainty.

'What are they?'

'They're in biology,' Alex answered.

'Oh,' Jonathan said. He thought for a moment. 'This place is weird,' he went on.

Hanging above the mantelpiece was a huge Marlin that Sam's father had caught on holiday at Key West. Set into a plaque of wood, the skin of the fish was blue and silver and its one visible eye made Jonathan shiver.

Sam was opening his presents. 'Who gave me the fly gun? I've lost the card.'

'I did, you div,' Jason said.

He had fallen onto one side and resembled a half dead elephant.

'What happened to your hair?' Jason asked.

Jonathan had only just noticed it too. Sam normally

had brown curly hair all over. Now half his curls were blond.

'That looks kind of ridiculous,' he said.

Jason sat up smartly. 'I like it,' he said. 'Sam, you lookin' ready, man.'

Alex had rolled some gift wrap into a ball and was weaving it between the chairs neatly and without energy. He circuited the TV and then went round again. A couple of the girls had come to the party dressed in stretch pants and clingy tops. One of them lounged across the table – a redhead, chewing bubble gum. She was a next-door neighbour and had been there before.

Sam had put some heavy metal band onto his docked iPod. He clicked his fingers and tapped one foot up and down. Jonathan found the whole sound disgusting. He had his father's taste in music, which included The Beatles, The Who and even Bach. Sam didn't have rhythm. Jonathan couldn't understand how one of his closest friends could be tapping out of time. Sam was missing all the main guitar riffs and the drum solo.

Jason came off the sofa. 'Let's go!' he crowed. His voice blended expertly with the singer's. 'I can feel the pain, the power and I'm ready to devour . . .'

Jason was lunging in several directions and when he hit

the floor, the surface went quivering along with him. His cap shot off and landed in the middle of the girls. They giggled very loudly, sharing a private joke, and Jonathan couldn't help thinking how he and the other boys would have had a better time on their own. Girls together were stupid, especially these ones. They were as bad as Mia. Not an audition candidate amongst them! Bill Jones would have fired them on the spot. The tallest girl was staring at him as he took to the floor and Jonathan caught the words 'fattie' and 'show off' between tracks. Well, he didn't care. He was half the size of Jason and he was also the only boy who really knew how to dance.

Jason had begun to beat his chest and moan.

'He's mad,' said the girl with the bubble gum and then she stood back quickly because Jason put a fist up in front of her face.

'You don't talk now,' he growled.

Sam's mobile was ringing and the heavy metal music was suddenly turned off.

'Hi, Mum,' he said after a pause. Sam was grinning and walking around as he listened. Obviously she had all the news because he didn't talk much.

New York was the place to go, Sam had told them often, because it was an island and he liked heights. The bagels were fantastic too. His mum was OK. One day, Sam would be joining her.

Jonathan's eyes followed the flickerings in the orange lava lamp until he couldn't draw himself away.

'Here!' Sam was holding the mobile out towards him. 'My mum wants to talk to you,' he said.

Jonathan came out of his trance and was suddenly shy.

'Hi, honey,' said Sam's mother through the phone.

Jonathan tried to say hi back, but he didn't get a chance.

'I think it's wonderful you're in a show, sweetie,' she said and the words were echoing from those many miles away. 'Who wrote it?' She obviously knew everything about production. 'I was a Bond girl once,' she purred, 'and in two movies directed by Jack Adams.'

There was more chat until the line began to fade along with Sam's mother. Jonathan breathed a sign of relief.

'She came out of the sea in a fur bikini,' he said as he handed the mobile back to Sam.

'Mum used to be a film star,' Sam replied. 'Before I was born, though.'

'Turn the lights out! Turn the lights out!' shrieked Jason

Someone was bringing the cake in covered with lit candles. After they had sung 'Happy Birthday', Sam shut his eyes and made a wish. Jonathan knew it was cheating but he had a wish too. Then they watched a cartoon on DVD.

Sam's father came downstairs. He ate most of the lettering on the cake and delivered a present that had aeroplanes on the wrapping paper.

'Everybody enjoying themselves?' he asked.

'Yup,' said Sam.

His father went back upstairs.

The girls had gone home when the kids realised that Sam wasn't with them any more. He had disappeared. Alex finally found him in the bathroom staring into the mirror. A half-open cupboard revealed a load of pills and toothpaste.

If you could get lost in a bath, this was the one to be lost in. The room was big with wide wooden floorboards. The colour scheme here was beige, even down to the back brush and scales.

'You don't take those pills, do you?' asked Alex.

The other boys were crowding round.

'I took a couple once,' Sam admitted. 'I think my mum swallows slimming pills quite a lot. She's always on a diet.'

Sam began to fold himself into the shower curtain until Jonathan could only see his knees bending through the plastic.

'Get out of there,' said Jason. 'You'll suffocate.' His lumbering frame tried to unravel Sam but it was no use.

The boy finally did a whirlwind turn back out of the curtain. Sam lifted his heavy head of hair right off his face. He looked younger than his twelve years.

'I think my mum and dad are making a big mistake,' he said.

Jonathan and Alex exchanged glances, and in that moment they shared the same sense of loss. Jonathan was happy that he had a job in the theatre. Most of his friends had decided to leave home as soon as possible. In the end, they were all agreed. It was the parents who let you down.

Chapter Eighteen

The next day, rehearsals were more chaotic than usual. Minutes stretched into hours as adult members of the cast came and went without any sense of urgency.

Bill's note-taking had reached legendary proportions. Did anybody care about the show? he muttered as he flung bits of paper around his seat in the auditorium. But even Bill was having difficulty in understanding where one scene ended and the next one began.

To make matters worse, Reg had developed the habit of playing unnecessary tunes. He and Bill were not speaking unless they had to and the friction between them was obvious.

The kids were in the middle of their flying carpet

parade. This wasn't a normal carpet. It consisted of a black cloth with stars painted across the width, which at the appropriate moment would be lifted by lines into the flies. Edging these lines were ultra violet lights that made everything sparkle. This was just a part of Sinbad's magical journey.

Miss Spencer was making sure the boys were grouping correctly. She had lost more weight and the veins in her hands rose separately like bones. Her practice skirt held no shape at all. Jonathan was certain that a puff of wind would blow her over.

'Move over to the left, Mia,' Miss Spencer ordered. 'You others get behind her.'

The children moved reluctantly until she got hold of one of the boys and put him in his place. 'Quick sharp,' she said.

'We wear culottes for this number,' Mia whispered. She had a trace of lipstick on and wouldn't stop moving about.

'Pay attention, Mia!' Miss Spencer said.

Jonathan didn't think she was in a very good mood. It occurred to him that Miss Spencer might be nervous too. He wondered how they would all be behaving in ninety-six hours. He stood on the spot and counted the hours again just to be sure he had got his calculation right.

'Jonathan!'

Now she was really angry.

'Sorry, Miss Spencer,' he said.

Reg's drumbeat persistently marked their routine on the carpet. The children had been through it so often now they were bored. They wanted instant costume and applause, not this repetitive stream of instructions.

Mrs Nathan was mouthing something to Mia from the wings. She had put her knitting down and tiptoed about as if she were waiting for her own entrance.

She tried again. 'I've got you a fizzy water, darling.'

Mia tried to ignore her mother. She turned away from her, shrugging her shoulders, now more intent on the exact placing of her steps.

'Your mother wants you.'

Tom was edging Mia towards the wings. His biceps rippled below his T-shirt and whenever he moved. He took the lion's share of the space.

A technician was trying to get past Mrs Nathan with a length of cable but she was in the middle of his path. He swore under his breath.

Seconds later, a voice came over the tannoy. 'Could we have anyone not involved in this scene off the stage, please?'

Mia had gone very red and the mole on her left cheek was all twitchy.

Jonathan had to admit that he preferred his own mum. Mrs Nathan was an embarrassment and he couldn't blame Mia for pretending that she wasn't there.

Miss Spencer had stopped the drum.

'Just a warning, children,' she said. 'Don't go too close to the pit or you'll fall over the edge of the stage. And never gaze directly into the strobes. After thirty seconds they could blind you.'

There was a hush. None of the kids had any idea that performing on stage could be so dangerous.

Mia put up her hand. 'I've looked longer than that,' she boasted, 'and –'

Miss Spencer cut Mia short. Her patience was wearing thin. 'That's quite enough. You haven't the experience to know.'

Tom nudged the other Parkview boys in the ribs and they nearly came off the carpet altogether.

When the rehearsal was at an end, the children had a break and some of them went off to an outside canteen. But Jonathan and Amy ate their sandwiches in the third row of the stalls. They wanted to stay and watch Zak and Cameron playing the camel.

The boys knew what they were supposed to do but they hadn't tried working under the frame. There was a lot of commotion when the two of them came on stage with their woolly legs on. Neither of them showed much enthusiasm for the part.

It took a couple of people to lift the frame over their heads. Zak took the front end and Cameron the back. But after they were covered and had taken a few unsteady steps in no particular direction, the camel collapsed.

Zak came out of the neckpiece, gulping air. 'It stinks in there!' he cried.

'Try again,' said Miss Spencer.

She pushed Zak back in and the camel began to shamble alarmingly downstage. The camel's name was Evangeline. She had one hump and gave a sly wink from under trailing eyelashes. Zak had pulled the right ring.

'Stop!' bellowed Bill. He was rubbing his gold chain like a series of worry beads. 'If you fall into the pit,' he said, 'we're going to have an insurance claim from the entire band.'

The camel was kicking. She took some sideways steps and stood bristling. Evangeline was potentially a violent creature.

'I don't think this is going to work,' Jonathan said to

Amy. He was glad he hadn't been chosen to be part of an animal.

'Nor do I,' Amy replied. 'D'you want some chocolate?'

Amy had her lunch neatly set out on silver foil which, when finished, would go into a plastic sachet with a zip. Everything about her was organised. She made Jonathan feel as though he carried too much luggage. Under the house lights, her eyes were clear and seemed to pierce him with the biggest pupils he had ever seen.

He knew he shouldn't eat chocolate. But Jonathan needed energy. He had broken the wrapper and was about to take his first bite when Bill interrupted him.

'I want this schedule taken to the Caliph,' he said, handing one of his notes to Jonathan. His tone conveyed disapproval. 'He's in his dressing room.'

Jonathan wished he were somewhere else and that he hadn't been caught with chocolate. It looked as if he wasn't trying to be slim.

On the stage, the boys were out of their camel costume and had now become involved in a heated exchange.

Cameron stood rubbing his lower spine. He was hot and bothered. 'You can't even walk straight,' he said to Zak, 'and you've got the easy part.'

Zak had turned away and was leaving the stage.

They had a long way to go as a team.

Jonathan knocked on the Caliph's door but there was no answer. He was about to push the paper underneath when it opened with a flourish.

'Come in,' said the Caliph. 'Whoever you are.'

'This is for you,' Jonathan said and gave him the note. If he was lucky, he could get away again and finish his chocolate bar in private.

The Caliph's hair was as black as shoe polish and pasted across his forehead. He appeared an even larger man close up, his wrinkles marking tributaries that fell away under the chin.

The Caliph was beckoning Jonathan to enter. 'Be careful. This place is so cramped, my mouse has got a hunchback.'

'Have you got a mouse in here?' asked Jonathan. He wanted to scream.

'Only a shy one,' replied the Caliph.

Behind him was a miniature TV featuring test cricket from Australia. Occasionally lines blurred the screen and took the players out of focus. Then the Caliph slapped the set and the game settled down again. A glass half filled with red wine stood on his dressing table.

'My creature comforts,' the Caliph explained.

Jonathan noticed that he wasn't limping any more. For someone so old, the Caliph appeared quite well.

'And what parts do you play in this production?' asked the Caliph. He in turn saw an overweight young boy who could have a nice smile if he tried. The boy was short but he had an air of curiosity about him that was fetching. In fact, he reminded the Caliph of himself many years ago.

Jonathan took a deep breath. 'I'm a sailor, a water sprite, a merchant, a courtier and an understudy.'

'That sounds like an awful lot to me,' said the Caliph.

'It is,' Jonathan replied. He went on. 'But I'm really a ballet dancer,' he confided.

'Good heavens, so was I once!' the Caliph said. 'So was I.' He peered at his reflection in the mirror and gave himself a kiss. 'There's nothing in the world like ballet,' he said.

Jonathan smiled then. He decided that the Caliph had to be OK.

The Caliph in turn lifted his glass and took another sip of wine, winking as he did so. 'Only keep that to yourself,' he said.

The sound of remote applause came from the TV. The commentator's voice had risen and the white baggy trousers of cricketers were ruffling in a light wind.

'People clapping ... that's what I like to hear,' said the Caliph. He had stopped looking at himself now and his expression was sad.

'There's nothing like it. Once the audience have taken you to their heart, the sky's the limit. You want more, until performing becomes an addiction and off you go then for the rest of your life. Do you understand what I mean?'

Jonathan looked gravely back at the Caliph. 'I think I do,' he said.

Chapter Nineteen

Later that afternoon, Tom and Princess Pearl finished rehearsing their duet, which was now complete. It made compelling watching and the scene met with Miss Spencer's approval.

Tom's full circle of the stage had brought him back to the cave entrance. He was panting but pleased to have achieved a non-stop run-through. Now he leant into a wall with his arms in a high V. Jonathan could see the sweat running down the back of his neck. The Princess sat as if abandoned by the script. But she had luck on her side. Prince Hassan was about to claim her.

From his position in the wings, Jonathan marvelled at the way Princess Pearl could play an actress and dance as well. She was able to stay *en pointe* in defiance of gravity with complete control. In a couple of years' time, Jonathan reckoned he would have the strength to lift a ballerina. Meanwhile, even Tom wasn't allowed to go that far. Neither he nor Jonathan were old enough yet.

'Are we done?' Pearl shouted across to Bill.

She was also dripping with sweat and there were damp patches all over her tunic top.

Bill put a thumb up and carried on talking to another member of the cast. Princess Pearl grabbed a towel and went off stage. Only Tom remained, marking out his territory and oblivious to the scene change going on around him.

The accident happened at four-thirty p.m. without warning. One moment, Tom was upright and there for everyone to see. In the next, he had gone, disappearing under a falling flat that was not properly weighted. The accompanying crash was horrific and Tom tore straight through the canvas. He had had no chance to move. A cloud of debris and dust rose as the flat crashed over him.

There was a great gasp from the crew and then they moved forward. Events after that were swift. The scenery was lifted and Tom at last appeared, very white and still. Miss Spencer knelt beside him. He was in shock.

'I can't move my legs,' he whispered.

Tom's body seemed drained of life. To Jonathan, who hovered on the edge, he had lost everything and lay like a dead person. It was frightening. Tom spoke in a small voice. Jonathan could see that he was shaking, either from fear or from being cold.

'Don't try to do anything,' Miss Spencer said.

Someone had already phoned for an ambulance. Miss Spencer stroked Tom's forehead. He had his eyes shut. He was whimpering in the way of a child.

The medics came fast and the stage was cleared while they made Tom comfortable and placed him on a stretcher. Outside the dressing rooms, Jonathan watched as the men in green came past with Tom laid out between them. They were going out to the ambulance.

He felt some strange and unexpected fellowship for the boy with whom he had worked so closely. Their competitive streak was somewhere in the past. Jonathan didn't hesitate and walked alongside the stretcher, and put out his hand to touch Tom's. The boy gave an answering squeeze.

'You'll be all right,' Jonathan said. He wanted to reassure him.

'Mind, son.'

The men were only doing their job and Jonathan was an obstacle. He felt himself pushed rudely into the wall. Tom's eyes had closed again but he seemed reluctant to let go of Jonathan's hand. As they came to the swing doors and out into the open air, Jonathan wanted to halt the procession. It was as though he was losing a friend.

They were beyond him now and making a difficult path outside. Snow here had fallen several centimetres deep and the ground was slippery.

'I'll come and visit,' shouted Jonathan.

He felt close to tears but he couldn't understand why. His chief competitor might end up on crutches. An image of 'Cheekbones Tom' laid low was something he couldn't at present begin to contemplate.

In the solitude of the passage, Jonathan had visions of the accident replaying so that the crackling statement over the tannoy passed him by. Jonathan wanted to be away from there. He wondered whether Tom would ever dance, or for that matter even walk, again.

The tannoy kept going. Jonathan was aware of his name being called with a degree of urgency. He couldn't wait any longer. In fact, as he came back up the stairs, he was glad of having a command to follow.

* * *

On stage, the atmosphere was tense. Bill Jones and Miss Spencer stood together discussing the future in low voices.

'There you are,' Miss Spencer said.

She looked worried. Bill was pacing the floor. Every time he reached a certain point, he turned and made the same number of steps back. Otherwise, the theatre was deserted. It was as if the entire cast had mysteriously gone to ground and left the three of them to their fate.

Bill was muttering. 'I don't think we can take the risk,' he said.

Jonathan crossed his legs for something to do. He was uncomfortable waiting like this.

There was more muttering, chiefly from Miss Spencer. She was disagreeing with Bill and shaking her head. Finally, there was a long pause in which they evaluated the situation. Then Bill nodded. He was weary and his shoulders drooped.

Jonathan stood stiffly. He wasn't good at predictions.

'You're to take over Tom's role,' Miss Spencer said. She was stern and yet encouraging at the same time.

Jonathan breathed again. 'Me?!' he squeaked.

Miss Spencer smiled. 'That's what an understudy is for,' she replied. 'But I didn't th-think that I'd ever h-have to really go on.' Jonathan knew that he was stammering. The temperature had dropped and colours collided in front of him. Nothing felt real.

'Go home,' Miss Spencer advised. 'Get some rest and we'll start tomorrow morning at nine-thirty sharp.'

Bill hadn't spoken during this exchange. Now he went off abruptly, swinging over the edge of the stage and disappearing into the pit.

The piano was playing, at first softly but becoming more insistent. Then the chords came at intervals. They were meant to stop anyone passing in their tracks.

'Shut it!' bellowed Bill from a low place.

There was quiet again.

Jonathan found himself outside the dressing rooms without knowing how he had got there. His actions were purely mechanical. He could hear the Parkview boys talking from behind the door of room number five and hesitated.

'One of us should have got the part . . . at least we're nearly the same size.'

Jonathan recognised Zak at his most aggressive. As he spoke, there was the sound of a box being pushed off a table.

'Yeah!' said one of the other boys.

'I want to dance with the Princess. He's going to look really sad up against her.'

'Is Tom going to die?' asked Cameron. He was further away.

'No,' Zak said. 'He's got a destiny. He told me so and I believe him.'

Jonathan pushed the door open. 'Hi,' he said.

'Hi,' the boys replied together.

Zak was washing his bright red, freckled face. Cameron looked for something in his tote bag impossible to find.

'Congratulations,' Zak said stiffly.

'Thanks,' answered Jonathan. He picked up his gear and went stumbling for his jacket. He felt numb.

Mrs Nathan and Mia were waiting at the stage door. Jonathan could tell that Mia was being sulky. She had obviously just heard the news. Mrs Nathan knotted her daughter's scarf around her neck but she wouldn't stay still. Mia turned away to finger squiggly outlines on the windowpane. Her silent combat was unnerving.

'I say, Jonathan,' Mrs Nathan said, 'your mother will be pleased . . . It's all very exciting, isn't it?'

'Yup,' said Jonathan.

Mrs Nathan patted her daughter's head comfortingly.

'Stop it,' said Mia, partly through her scarf.

Mrs Nathan sighed. She was buttoned up in a coat that bore traces of the same dog hair that had gone all over Jonathan. In fact, Mrs Nathan smelt of dog.

Mia was staring intently out of the window now. She pressed her nose against the stage door window that was cloudy with her own breath.

'Your dad's here,' she announced. Mia moved back.

If this was a joke, Jonathan thought savagely, he would kill her. But his heart was pounding again and he was pinned to the spot, as if he might stay right there for the rest of his life.

The bolt of the stage doors flew open suddenly. Jonathan saw his dad and he wanted to smile. His father was thinner and had obviously been through a period of starvation. He hadn't slept much either judging from the circles round his eyes.

Then Mr Morrison was reaching out to Jonathan and hugging him as if he would never let go.

'I'm home,' he said. His voice sounded unsteady.

'For good?' asked Jonathan. He must have things clear.

'I've missed you,' said his dad.

Chapter Twenty

Mrs Morrison cooked a feast that evening. The family ate roast chicken and potatoes with sweetcorn, cauliflower and white sauce. Jonathan scraped his plate for the very last mouthful. He couldn't understand why he had such an appetite and this bothered him. But the dessert of pecan pie and ice cream was very tempting. Jonathan had two helpings. Now he was really relaxed and could forget about tomorrow.

Dad's leaving and then coming back was OK if they could celebrate like this, Jonathan decided. His parents, thank goodness, were at last communicating.

Mrs Morrison had lit a candle, which wavered in the middle of the kitchen table. As the flame cast gentle shadows over the walls, their surroundings became another place. Charmian and Peter sat opposite one another, touching briefly at intervals. There was no sense of hurrying or of going anywhere. Jonathan's mother had a look on her face that bore all the sweetness of a homecoming.

Mr Morrison began to tell Jonathan about his own mother. He had never discussed his childhood before, only to mention in passing that he had been left on his own at a very young age. Jonathan had always believed that his grandmother had died early.

'So she was a dancer!' he said amazed.

'Yes,' replied his dad. 'She was a very talented dancer and my father wanted her to give up the theatre. When she had me, she was torn between her maternal instincts and her need to perform. What I never knew was . . .' Mr Morrison hesitated '. . . that she was still alive until last month.'

'Wow!' Jonathan said.

The story was better than a book or even a film on TV. And it was true.

'Why did reading about her death make you want to leave home?' asked Jonathan.

'The shock was so great, I didn't know what I was doing.

I went to visit my father's grave almost instinctively, and when I saw their names engraved next to one another, it made me understand everything.'

Mr Morrison's reflections were obviously painful to him.

'I was selfish,' he said. 'But I had to be on my own.'

Jonathan stuck out his lower lip. 'Mum says you went because you had lost your job.'

'Shush, love,' Mrs Morrison said. She turned away from the dinner table as water spouted from the kitchen tap.

Mr Morrison ground the salt cellar with his hands, and as he did so, little trails of white fell onto the table.

'No, not because of that,' he answered rather sharply. 'Your mother didn't know what had happened . . . I was always coming back, you know.'

Jonathan wondered how late it was. The events of the day were beginning to steal up on him again. He had another vision of Tom's face, pale and tragic as the ambulance men left the theatre. Then all the implications of the accident caused him to groan inwardly.

He tried to concentrate. 'But she doesn't look like you, Dad.'

Mr Morrison paused. 'I don't know . . .' he said. 'I was

young and slim once, though I never had ambitions to be a dancer.'

'You're not a theatre person,' said Jonathan. He didn't want to be rude, but he was quite sure of this. Jonathan still couldn't make any real connection between the newspaper photo of the lady called Michelle Kavinska and his father. How could they be related?

Mrs Morrison went upstairs. Perhaps she had a reason for leaving them alone. This was the first time Jonathan had had a really private conversation with his dad. There was one thing he was sure of: they wouldn't be discussing art or the EU.

From far beyond the hut and further than he could ever see came the sound of another train hurtling deeper into the countryside. Jonathan was glad that his parents were ready to chill. He needed peace and quiet. It worried him that he was so busy and he had a lot to take in.

'Why didn't you tell me she was a dancer, Dad?'

Jonathan could never leave things alone. Again his father recognised the tenacious streak that was so much a part of him too. An inherited trait . . .

'I'm sorry,' he said. His guilt at what he had done was bitter in him.

'I'll be just as good,' said Jonathan in a small voice.

He was pleading for his own cause, and now, he had no need to.

There came a moment where Mr Morrison surveyed his own life up until these last terrible weeks. He had failed as a father, that was for sure, and he had to make up for the time spent apart from them. Perhaps Jonathan had the talent . . . more, anyway, than he himself had ever shown as a recorder player in the school orchestra.

With the history of his own mother, Jonathan's attraction to the theatre was hardly surprising. No, Mr Morrison couldn't make any more mistakes. Family life on this December night was very dear to him.

He swallowed hard. 'I think that whatever you decide to do, you'll do very well,' he said.

'I won't!' choked Jonathan.

Tears were falling down his cheeks suddenly. As he brushed them away with the back of his hand, they came in a further rush and his nose felt wet.

'I've got to take over Tom's role and I can't do all the steps and his friends hate me . . .' Jonathan's fringe was flopping forward in a frenzy. His mouth quivered.

'I'm going to tell Miss Spencer tomorrow that my private maths has got in the way . . . and I don't have time for rehearsals.' He was still sobbing, but slower and with little grunts in between.

Mr Morrison laughed out loud. 'Well, that would be a lie, wouldn't it?' he said.

'Yes,' answered Jonathan, though he was too tired to be sure. Right now, he wouldn't have minded becoming a famous mathematician. He shouldn't have eaten all those potatoes. They weren't going to help his lift off. Nureyev had probably starved with real discipline the week before his big performances.

'You've got to remember the fact that there's dance in your genes,' his father remarked. 'You've got the stars on your horizon whether you like it or not.'

'That's what the wardrobe mistress told me,' Jonathan said. He was sitting up again and hopeful.

'Go to bed,' said Mr Morrison.

Jonathan didn't want to kiss his dad goodnight, so he gave him a bear hug that lasted for several seconds.

'See you,' he said as he went out of the room.

Mr Morrison sat on until the candle had dwindled to a smoky residue. The room was quiet. Charmian would be waiting for him. For the first time in months, Peter was happy.

Jonathan lay in bed with Barnaby on his duvet. After

a series of nocturnal squeakings, the guinea pig had snoozed off. Jonathan knew that he would be in trouble if his mum found out but he didn't care. He had been through enough today to need the company.

When she came in, Jonathan pretended to be asleep. The light from the passage burnt through his eyelids. Keep still, he prayed to Barnaby and the guinea pig did.

Mrs Morrison moved closer to the bed and then stopped. She didn't want to disturb Jonathan. As the door shut, her scent lingered in the room.

Jonathan was beyond sleep. His head throbbed. In the middle of the night and with the curtains closed, his problems seemed great. How would he remember all his entrances? Did the Moncrieff dancer know she was to have a new partner and would Amy still be his friend?

There were three days left to *Sinbad's* first performance. Jonathan could invent an excuse of maths as he'd suggested to Dad, though Hugs Bugs had stopped teaching now until the New Year. He wasn't much good at lying. Maybe he would get lucky and develop appendicitis.

Finally, Jonathan drifted into a troubled world of semi-consciousness. He had another dream. He was blindfolded and standing on the deck of a ship in a storm. His clothes were soaking and his hands were tied behind his back.

'Take the blindfold off,' shouted a voice. It was the Caliph speaking.

When Jonathan could see, he was surrounded on all sides by sailors. They were a grim lot and drunk on cans of lager. Reg was playing a grand piano under the flap of the mainsail, but the instrument appeared to be sinking. The men ignored him. They were more interested in Jonathan.

'Make him walk!' yelled a nasty brute missing his front teeth.

'Yeah, make him walk!' called everybody else.

The decision had already been made.

The Caliph raised a long whip high above him and then cracked it down onto the deck so that the surface sprang under Jonathan's feet. He was being led along the port side. As he passed the Caliph by, the man spoke softly so as not to be heard. 'Good luck, son.'

Walking the plank was a slow business. Jonathan tried to retreat but the tip of somebody's sword kept digging at his rear end. When he reached the edge and peered over, serpents rose hissing out of the depths of the ocean.

'Help!' screamed Jonathan.

He woke up in a sweat and was still full of fear.

'It's all right, you've had a bad dream,' said his father.

Mr Morrison had put on the overhead light and Jonathan blinked his way into the present. The guinea pig moved reassuringly on a damp patch in the folds of his duvet. This was a clear sign that they were all alive.

'I nearly drowned,' Jonathan said. 'I really did.'

Chapter Twenty-One

When the Caliph came on stage in full costume the next day, he was no longer the object of derision but a potentate of the East to be much admired.

Gone were the sticking plaster hair and the walking stick. Any sign of gout had been replaced by a stroll that put the fear of God into lesser mortals. The Caliph wore his clothes, which included a gold cummerbund, as if by divine right. His harem pants were laden with jewels and his pointed slippers tapered off into the air. They were called babouches.

The Caliph knew how to create a buzz of excitement. He was well in advance of the dress rehearsal.

'Look at him!' said Amy. 'Look at all those rubies.'

She and three other kids were waiting for their entrance in the left wing.

The Caliph gave a bow, brandishing his cutlass at the same time, which waved menacingly as a symbol of power.

Mia had pushed Amy aside to get a better view. 'They're fake, stupid,' she said. With her hands on her hips, she was conscious of her superior knowledge. 'I know all about jewellery because I've got a ruby brooch.'

'Quiet, girls,' Miss Spencer whispered. She was busy treading down some floor tape that had come unstuck.

The Caliph strode across the stage as the Wazir gave him his customary greeting.

'Welcome to the Peacock of the Silver Path, the Lion of the Golden Throne, the Ruler of the World, the Descendant of the Prophet, Haroun al Rashid, Ibn Abdullah, Ibn Abbas, Ibn Majomet – the Caliph!'

'Off you go, girls,' said Miss Spencer.

Mia, Amy and the other two ran to greet the Caliph in a line and then gave him their deepest curtsies.

He bowed again and waved them away. They came off stage.

'That's a long name,' Mia said.

'Be quiet!' Miss Spencer snapped. 'You won't hear your next cue.'

The Caliph was circling the stage slowly and as he did so, the bosun and various crew members of the boat followed at a respectable distance.

'Well, your ship is looking very trim, Mr Bosun, despite the discovery of a stowaway,' the Caliph said.

He stopped. He had been talking to thin air.

'Where is Sinbad?!' the Caliph shouted.

A call went through the tannoy. 'SINBAD . . . Sinbad to come on stage immediately.'

'I know where he is,' Mia said to Miss Spencer. She was almost coy. 'He's on his mobile by the props room. I just saw him.'

Miss Spencer gave an inward sigh. Illness had not done much to preserve her patience. 'Thank you for that information, Mia,' she said. She signalled to Bill who was downstage and waiting. 'He's by the props room!'

Bill had just written something down in capital letters in his notebook. He acknowledged her with a faint nod. He was working out the approximate time of various scene changes and also whether the children would get sufficient breaks between their last rehearsal and the first show.

'We'll go from the beginning of Scene Three,' he

called. 'I want to do a run-through of walking the plank.'

Jonathan, who was sitting in the stalls, felt faint. 'Oh, no,' he said.

But nobody heard him.

His dream had been a premonition. He was certain. OK, the real thing couldn't be that bad but it could still be bad enough. Now that he had a leading part, he could expect disaster.

Jonathan took up his script again and went through the additional pages that now involved him.

Technicians were shunting scenery back and forth. As the boat came down, a couple of men pushed a wooden stern into view. On the port side was a built-in plank that hung several feet out to sea.

That's where I was, thought Jonathan gloomily. He couldn't get that awful walk out of his head.

'Right, here I am,' announced Sinbad. He had appeared suddenly. In contrast to the Caliph, he wore dirty jeans and a sweater. 'Sorry, folks,' he said.

'Let's get a move on,' said Bill Jones. He began to turn his gold chain first one way and then the other. He bent towards his assistant and gave her some directions to pass on to Reg.

'Where've you been?' asked the Caliph. He had put

his cutlass in the corner and was waiting for something to happen.

'Had a bet on the dogs at Crayford and was just checking my quid's worth with the bookie.'

'Excellent,' said the Caliph. 'That will be worth a wee dram later.'

The girls were sitting in the wings. Their delays were usually associated with actors being late. It was what being in the theatre was about.

Mia yawned with a display of her tonsils. 'How naughty,' she said. 'My mum says that betting is much worse now the lottery gives out so much money. She says that most men are born to gamble.'

Mia closed her eyes as if for a snooze. 'I know what I'd like if I won . . .' she said dreamily. 'I'd have a leather jacket, a spa weekend and salsa dancing lessons in Cuba.'

Amy folded her arms and thought hard. She was enjoying the market scene and being Jonathan's wife, but she would never let on. 'I'd like the pantomime to be true to life,' she said.

'That's stupid,' murmured Mia. 'You can't buy a true-to-life pantomime.'

Sinbad had finally managed to squeeze through a porthole and stood unhappily in the middle of the plank. 'Am I insured for this?' he asked, shading his eyes anxiously.

'Course you are,' said the Caliph. He waved his arm.

Sinbad's next speech was not promising. 'By Allah,' he cried, 'this is an abominable way to go! Would to Heaven I had died a decent death and been washed and shrouded like a proper man!'

There was silence.

'Bill?' called Sinbad. He was desperate. 'Couldn't I have someone just behind me? I'm unstable up here.'

The Caliph was disgusted. 'This isn't Noah's Ark,' he said. 'Anyway, you get off in a jiffy.'

Bill wasn't rising to the occasion. He sat grim-faced and waiting, with a cup of coffee on his seat rest.

Prince Hassan entered for a big speech.

'He is innocent! Bring my dearest friend back from the brink. I am lost without him in my search for the diamond. If he dies, we are sunk and I will never have the hand of your lovely daughter, Princess Pearl.'

Prince Hassan, son of the Sultan of Morocco, went down on his knees.

'Captain, Sinbad was hungry and stole all the sausage rolls. What is more, I shared them with him. His own boat was taken by bandits. I beg of you, spare him.'

'Come aboard,' the Caliph said quite cheerfully. He took a short walk round the deck. 'Go search for the diamond Moor-El-Din. It is as big as a peacock's egg! But remember . . .' The Caliph paused. 'If you find the diamond, I will accept your dowry happily . . . Though he who marries a girl in a yashmak cannot afterwards ask for his cash back.'

The Wazir stepped out onto the plank and took Sinbad by the arm. 'The will of the Caliph is the will of Allah,' he declared.

Sinbad was sweating profusely. He seemed to be having a crisis. 'Thank God that's over,' he said. 'I never did develop a head for heights.'

The Caliph was adjusting his cummerbund. He nodded sadly at his friend. 'Pull yourself together,' he said. 'This is really pathetic behaviour.'

Mia had come to with a start and was leaning across Amy. 'If they're Muslims, they don't eat sausages,' she said.

'This isn't real life,' answered Amy sweetly and she was sorry that Jonathan wasn't there to hear her talk back.

Sinbad was descending with the help of a crew member but the business was slow. 'And a jolly good thing too!' he shouted.

From the wings came the sound of a dog barking. Her owner's voice was not far behind. With a yelp and her tail between her legs, Dottie skulked onto the stage. There she waited, growling all the while and showing the whites of her eyes.

The wardrobe mistress had lost control.

'You nortie, nortie dog . . . I tak you away.' The woman was obviously in some distress. She had raised her shawl above her head where it hung like a redundant flag. 'Nortie, nortie . . .' she said again.

Bill and the rest of the cast were looking at the two of them in amazement. The dog had settled down and was licking her hindquarters. Dottie didn't mind who witnessed the scene. She was safer with other people there.

'Could you please move your dog, Olga?' requested Bill. 'She's a damn nuisance.' He was tapping his pen impatiently.

Olga turned towards the Caliph and wrung her hands in despair. 'Please don be cross. Dottie mak a mess . . . I cleer everytink up . . .'

The Caliph wasn't moving. 'What do you mean, she's made a mess?' he asked. 'You mean, she's made a mess on something of mine, is that it?'

The wardrobe mistress put the shawl about her shoulders and tried a shrug that was casual. 'She hav a tuch of tummy trubble. She hav an accident on yor coat in the dressing room.'

The entire theatre had gone quiet. Nobody spoke. The Caliph's complexion was as red as his turban. His neck seemed to be expanding and he swallowed several times.

A storm was about to break.

Chapter Twenty-Two

The Caliph's few words to Dottie had an immediate effect. The poodle, whose top knot rose like a stalk several centimetres into the air, was already languishing. She gave a whine of great distress and then went off in the guise of a smaller animal. The engagement was over.

The Caliph turned to Olga. 'If that dog comes anywhere near me again, I take no responsibility for what might happen. For her own safety, I suggest you keep her on a lead.'

The wardrobe mistress was angry too. She shared a home with Dottie and episodes such as this took place on a regular basis. 'She is jus a leetle dog . . . She is getting on now and she as a weak bladder.'

'All the more reason for not bringing her into the theatre!' The Caliph had removed his turban in the heat of the moment.

Suddenly, Bill was between the two of them and holding up his hand. 'Olga,' he said, 'the Caliph has a point. We can't let your dog go around making messes everywhere. If she isn't well, she should stay in your house.'

Olga stared mournfully ahead of her. 'Dottie cry all de time when she is alone,' she replied. 'Then I cry . . .'

Bill was muttering something unintelligible. 'All right,' he said to the cast who were still waiting. 'Half an hour's break while we sort this out.'

The wardrobe mistress had fallen into a heap at the side of the stage and was sobbing loudly. Her shawl was flung across her face, as if she were in hiding. Once she sat up and made a declaration to the gods. 'I am being persecuted . . .' she cried. 'Vot is happening to me and the other refugees in this country?'

The Caliph stood over her. He wasn't sympathetic. 'I don't know, dear, but I'm going to the Cock and Pheasant to have a think about it.'

The dog was nowhere to be seen. Sinbad had left the stage and now the Wazir and the Caliph were moving off too.

Jonathan felt sorry for Olga, even though she had frightened him in the wardrobe room. 'Do you think she's lonely?' he asked Mia as they came down the stairs together.

Backstage, the gloom was intense and Jonathan wondered briefly whether snow had begun to fall again.

'Who . . . the dog?'

'Don't be stupid,' said Jonathan.

Through the murky half-light, Mia was a dark figure tripping next to him. Very soon, they would be in the glare of spotlights with no hiding place to turn to. At this dreadful thought, Jonathan shivered.

The day was difficult. After a run-through of some of the main speeches, Bill was left shaking his head in disbelief. They were far from performance standard, so he told the cast. Any dynamic edge was entirely absent.

Unfortunately, the leads had played this panto before. Most of them were saving their energy for later.

The Caliph's return from the pub, accompanied by Sinbad, the Wazir and Prince Hassan, was a shaky one. In fact, the Caliph had a problem standing upright and was sent home in a taxi. Entire scenes were put on hold.

Now the stage was empty apart from Jonathan and

the Moncrieff dancer. Everyone else, including Bill Jones, had left the theatre.

His moment had come. As Miss Spencer bent to press the *play* button on the CD player, Jonathan was aware for the first time of being close to a live ballerina. She seemed quite friendly. In fact, she was smiling at him now as she did the splits. Her legs were those of an acrobat.

The trouble was, and Jonathan couldn't bear to admit it, Princess Pearl was taller than he was. Only by a head, but that would definitely make a difference. He wondered whether people would laugh when they saw the two of them working side by side.

'This way, Jonathan.'

The Old Man of the Sea had been fought off seconds before. This was Jonathan's chance to show himself. Miss Spencer was leading him in a wide circle only to draw backwards with four grand steps and an arm wave, as if greeting a far-off friend. Princess Pearl had got up from the floor and now ran helter-skelter, ending with a *pirouette en pointe*. As she finished her turn, she was next to Jonathan.

'Take her hand,' Miss Spencer told him, and the Princess held his quite firmly when they ran again in a smaller circle.

Miss Spencer was panting. Both the women were.

'Pearl's *pirouette* is the music cue, and then you start to move, Jonathan,' she said. 'Don't forget that your entrance has to be grand and stately. You set the mood, Jonathan. By the end of the duet, Princess Pearl comes face to face with Prince Hassan, her husband to be. You are the courier, as it were, and passing her into his further care.'

'Oh,' said Jonathan.

What a pity their *pas de deux* had to end like this. He was resigned to the fact that he couldn't play the romantic lead. Anyway, that would have been too hilarious for his mates at school. Them being there and watching the performance was going to be bad enough.

Miss Spencer was leaning against a speaker for support. She took slow hoarse breaths that made Jonathan want to help her. But he didn't know how.

'Try that on your own,' she suggested.

Miss Spencer's lips were blue. Was she going to collapse?

But he had no time to wonder. The CD was back on and Jonathan was forced to concentrate. When he came to take the Princess's hand, he found it light and reassuring. She reminded him of a bird flying off into the sky.

Princess Pearl was as close now as she would ever get

to him. Briefly, Jonathan let his eyes wander to where her bosoms should be under the leotard. With a shock, he realised that she didn't have any. Unlike his mum, the Princess was flat-chested.

She was following on with a series of half jumps and slides. A horn played an eerie tune and the dancer lifted her right leg into an *arabesque*, which she held for a number of bars.

'Now, Jonathan,' ordered Miss Spencer.

She placed her hands on top of his and guided them to the Princess's waist. The Princess then *chasseed* diagonally across the floor with Jonathan just behind and still holding on to her. He was happy to be placed here and out of sight. When the Princess came to do a double *pirouette en pointe*, Miss Spencer held his hands again so that they supported her as she turned. With his help, she couldn't fall over.

At the end of the *pas de deux*, Jonathan and Princess Pearl drifted apart. The next chords would signal the moment where Prince Hassan entered and Jonathan went off stage.

'Let's see the whole thing,' Miss Spencer said. The vital spirit had come back to her just the same.

Jonathan found the second run a cinch. He didn't have

to do much other than be there for Princess Pearl when she was *en pointe*. He was becoming used to the close-up encounters. When she had gone from him, Jonathan found himself unexpectedly sad.

'Good,' said Miss Spencer as they came to the end.

Jonathan allowed himself a backward look at the Princess, who would fall straight into the arms of Prince Hassan. In a few years' time, if he lost a bit of weight and all went well, Jonathan would be stepping out as a prince in his own right.

'One more run-through, Jonathan?' Miss Spencer's colour had returned and she was his teacher, as normal.

'I'm a bit tired,' he replied.

Miss Spencer was smiling now, confident that the pair had made a bond to secure their work. 'You're doing fine. Just keep everything as it is,' she said as they went off stage.

At her departure, Jonathan felt an urge to protect Miss Spencer as well as Princess Pearl. He wondered whether his teacher had anybody to love.

The wardrobe mistress came face to face with Jonathan outside the Caliph's dressing room. She carried a cloth and a bottle of disinfectant.

'He iz a beastly man,' Olga announced, 'and I av

cleaned hiz room so hard, he vill be sick with the stench. Serves him right.'

Jonathan didn't answer.

Olga peered at him through an enveloping smell. 'So,' she said, 'the boy with the stars . . .'

The cloth had dropped to the floor but Olga didn't notice. She was about to make another prophecy.

'Yor family hav a white car?' she asked.

'No, a red one,' said Jonathan. 'A Volvo estate.'

'Yor family hav trubble with the car, mark my words,' Olga went on.

'We already do,' replied Jonathan.

He wanted to get out of his practice clothes and meet his dad, who would be waiting for him. If Jonathan stayed around much longer, he would have to keep a sleeping bag at the theatre.

The dog was dragging Olga's cloth out of reach, only to attack it. Dottie pointed her nose straight at Jonathan and kept up a monotonous growl. Her poodle coat was in need of replacement.

'Nortie, nortie dog,' said Olga. She bent down to pat her.

Dottie bared her teeth. To Jonathan, she was a horrible animal and needed a dentist.

Chapter Twenty-Three

Snow again. The weather forecasters had given their predictions correctly. This was a winter with the lowest temperature on record, and as further flurries fell from the skies, even outdoor animals sought shelter. Houses became shapeless, developing turrets that had not been there before. Children tobogganed in the streets.

The doctors' afternoon surgery on the west side of town was busy. Three receptionists at the desk dealt with a stream of appointments. In a confined playpen, toddlers went up and down on the rocking horse that squeaked. Adult patients either read magazines or peered vacantly ahead.

Miss Spencer watched the comings and goings as if

from a distance. The thump of her heart beat irregularly. She was alone.

'You're next!' A woman was digging into her ribs.

Miss Spencer got up stiffly and went to the door of her doctor's room. As usual, his table overflowed with medical files and pieces of paper. She sighed. He was a most untidy man.

'Take a seat,' the doctor said.

Miss Spencer sat straight in a chair while he peered at his computer screen. That and the waiting generally only added to her irritation. The doctor then put a note in his diary and turned to meet her gaze.

The tone was matter of fact. 'We've got your X-rays.' The doctor coughed as though he had some obstruction in his throat.

'Tell me the truth,' Miss Spencer said.

A block of ice had dislodged from a pipe somewhere above them and fell with a bump onto the road beneath. Blinds half-drawn across the windows were bunching, held by double strings that knotted into a hook on the wall. The calendar's December page featured reindeer from Lapland.

'It's not good news,' the doctor said. 'You can see for yourself how the growth has spread . . .' He was standing now.

'No,' said Miss Spencer. 'I don't want to look at the X-rays. There's no need. Just give me the facts.'

A file fell off the doctor's desk. Then the telephone rang.

'Yes?' he queried into the receiver. 'Tell her I'll call back.'

There were children outside. The normal screams of young people enjoying themselves. Miss Spencer could not remember any sense of freedom in youth. Her career had been a meteoric rise to the top, the struggle to maintain perfection.

'You've got about two months,' the doctor said, 'possibly a bit longer. With remission . . . we could be talking six. I'm very sorry.'

Miss Spencer saw each object in the surgery clearly. The photograph of the doctor's wife holding their baby, a gaming cartoon and the closed files that recorded sickness and sorrow.

'I see,' she said.

She was calm. Confirmation of what she had dreaded for so long made her stronger. The mission ahead of her was clear, as if directed by God himself.

The doctor was checking his computer screen. 'The specialist is ready to see you at two-fifteen tomorrow.'

'No, thank you,' replied Miss Spencer.

She didn't want any more to do with them or their metal machines that couldn't make her better. The children were all important now and they needed her. Miss Spencer knew that she had to succeed and, as ballet mistress of *Sinbad*, nothing must distract her from the smooth running of the show.

'Are you a believer?' she asked the doctor.

He was embarrassed and shifted his legs under the table. 'No, I'm afraid not,' he answered.

'Do try,' was all she said.

Shortly after Miss Spencer's appointment, Mr and Mrs Morrison met in the new town patisserie. Charmian had managed to take a day away from the garden centre and her mobile was switched off. Relaxing over a cappuccino, she was unaware that the froth had made a film around her lips.

Peter loved his wife more than ever. 'Wipe your mouth,' he said.

He had waited for so long to give her good news. Now that he had something to tell Charmian, he hesitated.

Her hair was messily swept up in a comb. There were hints of grey amongst the blonde sweep but these only added to his sense of protection. Mr Morrison touched his wife's face and, as he drew closer, she visibly relaxed. Why did he still find it so hard to express his feelings for her without sounding ridiculous?

His wife was fixing him with an even stare as if she could guess his thoughts.

Mr Morrison came back to the present. 'I've been invited to Brussels to discuss my marketing proposal,' he said.

'What, that old fisheries policy?' Mrs Morrison tried not to sound incredulous.

'It's not old, love . . . This is about bringing fish stocks to sustainable levels by 2015 and how I can make it a viable proposal for the Spanish. I think I'm back in business.'

Peter took a bite of his chocolate torte cake. 'I'm booked to go for a few days after the New Year. If everything works out, I shall be working from both here and Brussels.'

Peter was excited. Charmian hadn't seen him like this for so long. Her husband was at last returning to his former self. A man of energy and ideas! That piece of paper she had found in his study with those crazy diagrams and drawings belonged to the past.

She kissed her husband's forehead. 'That means

Jonathan can go for serious dance training.'

Mr Morrison's frown was only fleeting. His mother's history could never be repeated. He wouldn't stand in Jonathan's way now. Peter scraped up the last crumbs of his cake.

'You're getting fat,' Charmian said.

'I know,' he replied.

People from the shopping arcade were crossing in front of the café. A woman stopped briefly and peered at a menu through the glass.

'That's Miss Spencer!' exclaimed Charmian. 'My goodness, doesn't she look ill?'

Peter saw her too. The sharp-edged features were sallow, her wrap loosely set about her shoulders. Up until now, she had been a figure only in his imagination. He was shocked that this major influence on his son could turn out to be so frail. Nor did she look the approachable type.

Had his mother ended her days that way? Peter wondered. Had she walked other anonymous streets with nowhere to go? And as he continued to stare out of the window, she was suddenly gone, as if she had been part of a dream all along.

'Let's go,' he said briskly.

The sky had turned to a midnight blue as the Morrisons left the café. Lights shone from shops open to last-minute shoppers, but up above them there were no stars.

Peter stopped outside a chemist's. He put his arms around Charmian and held her tightly, then kissed her for a long time.

'Stop it,' protested Charmian. She tried to make Peter walk on but he kept her near. 'We're in a public place and people are looking,' she said.

They were. A gang of boys who passed were making rude noises. One of them ate fish and chips from a plastic carton, refusing to give anything away to the smaller kid next to him.

'Look at them geezers snogging,' the first one said. 'They're old enough to be sixty.'

The smaller boy had run on towards the entrance of an amusement arcade. 'Oughtn't to be allowed,' he shouted. 'Disgusting, that's what I call it!'

Peter had stopped kissing Charmian.

'Oh dear,' she said. She wanted to laugh again but she didn't dare. Peter was striding ahead and pulling her with him.

'I don't look that old, do I?' he asked anxiously.

Charmian drew alongside him and put her hands on his face. 'To them we do,' she replied. 'When we reach a certain age, it will be nice not having to try to keep up with the young.'

The Morrisons began to walk up the hill. Very soon Peter was puffing and short of breath.

'For some of us, it's too late for that,' he said.

Chapter Twenty-Four

In deteriorating conditions, Mrs Nathan drove Mia and Jonathan home. At six-thirty p.m., the nose to bumper crawl out of town was at its worst and when they reached the motorway, white-coated cars made a ghostly passage. Even three-lane traffic was forced to slow down.

Mia sat in front, reading out loud the occasional celebrity interview from a fashion magazine. From the back seat, Jonathan was amazed at her casual attitude. He wished he could read something as well but his mind was too taken up with tomorrow's dress rehearsal. Of course if the snow thawed, there could be flooding . . . the opening night would then have to be postponed. If only . . .

'You'll ruin your eyesight, darling,' Mrs Nathan said,

glancing sideways at her daughter.

'Won't,' replied Mia.

Mrs Nathan tried again. 'I hear poor Tom has had a kneecap removed,' she said.

She was finally able to see out of her rear-view mirror with the aid of a cushion under her bottom. Jonathan noticed that Mrs Nathan's driving wasn't any different and that his passenger door was rattling.

Mia rolled up her magazine. 'It's called a patella,' she announced.

Jonathan wriggled his right kneecap from side to side. 'Mine moves,' he said.

'Of course it does, stupid,' said Mia. 'But you can learn to dance again without one. The hospital says that Tom will be back to normal in a year's time.' A gold-threaded scarf escaped from the fur collar of Mia's anorak. Her drop earrings swung with the motion of the car, little pink stones set in chunky hearts.

'How do you know?' Jonathan asked.

''Cause I talked to Bill, stupid, and I sent Tom a get-well card as well.'

'Don't keep calling Jonathan, stupid, darling. That's very unkind of you, especially when he has to take Tom's place in the show and everything.'

Mrs Nathan had moved into the middle lane without signalling. A loud hoot was joined by several others and these carried on until another car went past them on the outside. Even though it was dark, Jonathan could see three young boys in the back sticking out their tongues at Mrs Nathan.

'Road rage,' she said. 'I think people are dreadful nowadays. They have no manners at all.' Mrs Nathan pursed her lips grimly as she put her foot down on the clutch pedal.

Jonathan felt very guilty. Trust Mia to send a card to Tom first. How could he have forgotten? He would get an adult to escort him to a shop at the next rehearsal break he had.

Mia was fidgeting. She put one hand under her jaw and the other round her neck until something snapped.

'Darling, stop it,' Mrs Nathan said. 'We don't want any further injuries, now, do we?'

'That's a chiropractic move,' said Mia airily. 'I can work on anyone.' She turned round to grin at Jonathan. 'You too, podge,' she said.

Jonathan didn't reply. As well as Mia being so annoying, he had dog hairs up his nose.

Mrs Nathan didn't seem to be making much progress

on the motorway. In fact, she was slowing down.

'Mum!' Mia had screamed.

Lights were flashing all over the place. Suddenly the car took a sharp left and came off the road. Gravel spun under the wheels. Jonathan felt himself airborne and weightless and aware that events were happening beyond his control.

Finally he came down onto his side, but without much of a bump. He was to remember this only afterwards. Meanwhile, the crash was real enough and the sounds of breaking glass splintered noisily around him.

Then a silence.

When Jonathan thought it safe to open his eyes, he had no other view than the twigs of a holly bush in the headlights of Mrs Nathan's car.

'Wow!' he said.

He couldn't remember whether the Big Bang came before he was born or after he was dead, but whichever it was, Jonathan had to remain cool. Either way, and he hadn't lost his memory yet. The show would have to go on without him.

'Wakey, wakey,' said a figure from above.

Mia was peering in at him and standing upright. There wasn't much wrong with her at all.

The car had tipped forward but miraculously remained upright. Next to her daughter, Mrs Nathan couldn't speak a word. She was intent on finding some gesture of life from Jonathan.

'Where am I?' he asked groggily.

The seat belt was digging into him. Jonathan undid the clasp with difficulty and came out through the now open door. Then he sat down on the edge of a verge covered in lots of snow.

'Thank God!' moaned Mrs Nathan. She shook all over and her teeth were chattering. 'I'm so sorry,' she said. 'I'm so very sorry . . . I don't know what happened.'

Mia looked at her mother and then at Jonathan. 'Don't worry,' she said. 'I think Mum's going through the menopause.'

Mrs Nathan was crouching down now into an inert bundle. She was sobbing.

A forklift truck had come to a stop nearby and two men were stepping out towards them. Their ordeal was nearly over.

'Get up, Mum,' Mia said, and she put an arm out to help her.

The pace of traffic had become a distant whine. Jonathan was conscious of having wet trousers and that everything going on was in slow motion. He stared at the Nathan vehicle with mounting recognition.

'You've got a white car!' he said. He couldn't believe what he was seeing.

'So?' said Mia.

'Olga got the wrong family!' Jonathan exclaimed. 'She said we'd have trouble with our car, but it's red.'

The wardrobe mistress wasn't much of a fortune-teller. Jonathan would tell her so tomorrow. Right now he wanted to get home. He would have a bath and eat his dinner, which he had already decided was to be scrambled eggs and chips.

When they finally arrived at the Morrison house, Mrs Nathan had a large scotch and got driven away with Mia in a taxi.

The car had been towed off for repairs.

Mr Morrison drank several scotches himself and went red in the face. 'That woman is a menace to the roads!' he shouted. 'She's not driving my son anywhere ever again. We're lucky Jonathan's here in one piece.'

'I don't think it was her fault,' said Mrs Morrison tactfully.

Jonathan had eaten his scrambled eggs and chips and was watching an even worse car accident on the News.

'Not a decent female driver amongst you,' said Mr Morrison. His speech was beginning to slur. He walked about as though he might have somewhere to go.

'That's a very chauvinistic remark,' Mrs Morrison said. 'I know lots of awful male drivers. They're always going too fast on the motorway. Now don't let's make what could have been a serious situation worse. Anyway, Jonathan had his seat belt on, and don't forget that Mrs Nathan and I went all the way to Cornwall together last summer and everything was fine.'

'I haven't forgotten,' said Mr Morrison. 'Jonathan told me that Mrs Nathan had a problem overtaking an ice-cream van in Penzance.'

Mr Morrison fell into an armchair by mistake and groaned. 'You'll have to cancel your work at the garden centre until the *Sinbad* run is over,' he said. 'We're not letting Jonathan back in her car whatever happens.'

Mrs Morrison was about to protest when she caught sight of the accident on TV. In the pre-holiday rush, this had become a major pile up and she shuddered at the resulting chaos. Mrs Morrison could have cried then at Jonathan's lucky escape.

Jonathan was lying down with one shoulder buried into where the sofa divided in the middle. His face was relaxed considering what he had been through, the sweep of his fringe tangled and thick. Jonathan was up too late, as usual.

Their Christmas tree was nearly ready. Mrs Morrison had hung the nativity sheep and coloured balls so that they covered every branch. Peter's task would be to add the lights. She looked back at her husband in his chair, suddenly wanting his physical touch.

Mr Morrison's mouth had fallen open and he was snoring. Charmian marvelled that he could drop off so easily. She didn't really mind doing the drive to and from the theatre, because secretly she had had enough of the garden centre's surly accounts manager, and of cleaning the soil from under her fingernails. She was going to chuck the whole thing in soon when Peter started work. Hopefully, that wouldn't be too long.

Jonathan had left the sofa and was shaking his father. 'Wake up, Dad, you're snoring,' he said.

Mr Morrison kept his eyes shut. 'That's impossible,' he said. 'I'm awake.'

'No, you're not,' replied Jonathan. 'Well, you weren't a minute ago.'

Mr Morrison's jaw was slackening again. The snores began again even louder.

'He's useless,' Jonathan said. 'Mum, do something!'

Mrs Morrison patted her son on the head and gave a shrug. She had been trying for years. 'I wish I could,' she said.

Chapter Twenty-Five

Evangeline wouldn't budge. The camel had fallen back on her hind legs while her front ones were straining to go forward. She hovered in a very precarious state. Evangeline wasn't far from sitting on her tail.

'Nice coat,' said the vendor loudly. 'Good-natured too. She'll take you to your destination if you press the right pedal.'

Princess Pearl and her governess looked at Evangeline as if she were a foreign beast.

'We are aiming for the Valley of the Diamonds,' said Princess Pearl.

The vendor was optimistic. 'No trouble,' he said. 'No trouble at all.'

Evangeline had come up off her backside. She was on the go again. Her eyelashes were batting. Without warning, she veered sideways and fell straight into the wings.

'Cut!' said Bill Jones. 'Let me see the wretched pair of you before I go mental.'

Bill had little time left to make changes, but these unscheduled stops were delaying the production even further.

He groaned. Zak and Cameron had no idea of co-ordination and Bill was weary from lack of sleep.

There was chatter on stage where the traders had gathered. White tape marked certain areas as a guide so that the market scene was sufficiently populated.

'They weren't supposed to go off like that,' Jonathan said to Amy. He was not used to holding a tray of coconut oil and his arms ached. He wanted a sandwich.

Amy blew her nose while they waited. 'They don't get on,' she said in a muffled voice.

Zak and Cameron were now out of the frame and in front of Bill, both red in the face.

'He won't do what I tell him!' shouted Zak. 'And he keeps going the wrong way.'

'No, I don't!' Cameron shouted back.

'Quiet!' said Bill. He tugged at the chain around his

neck as if this action gave him some support.

Cameron mopped his eyes. 'I never wanted to be a camel, anyway,' he said.

The children were dispersing. They had been told to place themselves for the courtiers' scene. Jonathan was pleased. That meant a seat at the foot of the Caliph's throne without activity. His problem was having Mia sit next to him. Given the choice, he would have preferred Amy.

Jonathan's costume hung ready on a rail for later. His harem pants were now a perfect fit. The wardrobe mistress had finally chosen the silver ones with a blue flouncy shirt and Jonathan had to admit that, when fully kitted out, he was the right person for the job.

The Caliph had taken to his throne and the children who were courtiers waited patiently beneath him. Technicians checked the machine that gave off smoke, and stuck yet more tape down to establish exits and entrances.

'Come along, come along!' said the Caliph. He had had enough of this lark.

Sinbad's long face was appearing from behind a curtain in the wings. 'Is this me?' he called, but he seemed to know that it was and came to perch alongside the rest of them.

Prince Hassan was having a cloak altered for his final

ceremonial sweep with Princess Pearl. Other people were missing too. The place was a shambles. So long to wait, thought Jonathan as he glanced at his watch. There were just three hours until the dress rehearsal. He wanted to pee.

Mia had a piece of tied-up string drawn between her fingers and they moved restlessly, making loops. Jonathan wished she would stop it.

Downstage, Miss Spencer was directing Pearl into a series of fine *pirouettes*.

'Wow,' said Mia. 'Did you see that? I can do those. Only a bit slower.' Mia gazed at the Princess, stuck for further words.

For a moment, Jonathan had feelings of pride. As her partner for the duet, he would shortly be dancing with the Princess. Taking her hand . . . guiding other turns. Then the butterflies came back to him a million times worse than before. Jonathan wished he had a pill to calm him down.

'Would you care to get me a glass of water?' The Caliph was addressing Mia.

She sprung to attention, smiling coyly. It was about time he noticed her.

'Saucy little madam,' said Sinbad.

The Caliph bent towards Jonathan and whispered in

his ear. 'She's our Lady Muck, wouldn't you say?'

Jonathan wanted to giggle out loud but he didn't. He nodded instead.

'I hear a divorce between the two boys playing the camel is imminent,' the Caliph said to Sinbad.

'Oh?'

Jonathan listened hard.

'You've got no idea what goes on under a camel's coat, young man,' the Caliph said to him.

Sinbad was yawning. He needed a pint to get himself going. 'One of those, eh?' he laughed.

Bill was going over the score with Reg, who sat at the piano. There was to be a new introduction to the sailors' chorus, long enough to allow the crew to pull the boat into line. Reg turned his attention to the synthesiser and played all the sound effects of a storm. It was convincing.

'Fine,' said Bill. 'That's absolutely right.'

'Are you sure?' asked Reg. His left leg was shaking.

'Absolutely,' replied Bill, and he was gone again before Reg could say more.

Now Bill was appraising the talons of the Roc, a giant bird whose presence would be only half seen. These were attached to long spindly legs dangling menacingly from the heights. The bird was another adversary of Sinbad and Prince Hassan on their adventures.

At last the children were told to break.

Jonathan and Amy came down the stairs together but they said little. Only an hour and a half to go, and during that time the kids were supposed to eat and have a rest.

Mrs Morrison was waiting for Jonathan and Mia at the stage door with extra rations that she should have brought earlier. 'I thought you might like some chocolate,' she said.

Her son was not happy. He opened his replenished lunchbox and had a look at the contents.

'Energy food,' Mrs Morrison added quickly.

She had been waiting in the canteen opposite, having drunk three cups of coffee in succession. Her son's big engagement was getting to her too.

'All right, then,' said Jonathan. He would never forgive his mum for letting it happen.

The hairdresser had cut his hair earlier into the sort of pudding-basin style that resembled Friar Tuck. Now Jonathan had to suffer the consequences. He was under the impression that the whole cast were laughing at him.

'I'll pick you up at eight,' Mrs Morrison said.

From the next day onwards, performances were scheduled to begin at seven-thirty p.m. sharp.

The boys' dressing room was empty. Jonathan tried on his lycra shorts and ate a chocolate bar in private. He wondered what Zak and Cameron were doing and whether they were still quarrelling. They were exactly the same height, which made the two of them right to play the camel. That wasn't his fault. For once, Jonathan was glad that he was shorter than them.

He was busy thinking and hadn't noticed the two cards addressed to him, lying beside his hairbrush.

The first one was written in shaky handwriting and showed a picture of a rabbit holding balloons. Inside the message read:

> Dear Jonathan
> Good luck with the leeps
> YO
> Tom
>
> PS: I've had an operation and my leg is in plaster. Its very hot in here and I am thirsty. Too much shepherds pie. The kitchen is on strike.

Jonathan didn't know what to do. Here was a card all the way from Tom in hospital and he had still forgotten to buy him one in return.

How could he have been so dumb?

The other card was different. Boys playing football on the front, with the ominous words:

GOOD *lUCK*, JONATHAN
We will be in the front row
on *YOUR FIRST NIGHT*.
love from Alex, Jason, Sam, Marcus and all of Class 7

Oh no!

Jonathan stood the cards in front of his mirror. He was clammy under his armpits and he felt sick. How would he be able to perform with his school out there following every move?

This had to be the worst nightmare possible.

Jonathan was beside himself with worry. Then he spied a blanket on the open shelves. He took it down, covering himself up so that his body was hidden. Jonathan glared at his own reflection in the glass.

An angry boy looked back at him with plump cheeks and a lost dimple. However long Jonathan stayed this way, he was still Friar Tuck, and wearing a blanket.

Chapter Twenty-Six

The dress rehearsal took place with the addition of a four-piece band and an audience of six. As the kids said later, the show went off like a damp squib. *Sinbad* even started late because the wardrobe mistress hadn't delivered veils on time to the Caliph's court girls. After that, one mishap became a series.

During Scene Two, Prince Hassan lost the heel of his right boot and there was a collision halfway through the sailors' hornpipe.

Jonathan's hoist never arrived. That meant Jonathan had been left to improvise in the middle of an empty stage. As a last resort, he went waving to the right and then to the left, but those in the audience were onto him and they were tittering.

There was general disbelief that everything had gone so badly.

The men of the pantomime went to The Cock and Pheasant afterwards. Commiseration of some sort was needed.

Prince Hassan had developed a limp. 'I'll have a large gin and tonic with ice,' he said to the barman. He was going to spend time here.

The Caliph and Sinbad were already drinking in an alcove lit by a log fire. The post-mortem on what had just taken place was gloomy.

'Olga must be due for retirement soon,' said the Caliph. 'She's well past her sell-by date. I've never known a wardrobe mistress to forget whole costumes. And what happened to Hassan's boot?'

The Prince took a long sip from his glass before sitting back with a sigh. 'I don't know,' he said, 'but my cloak's as heavy as a sack of potatoes and I'm shattered.'

Sinbad contemplated his glass. 'The boat sequence went quite well, considering . . .' The uneven flicker of flames cast shadows on his face giving him the appearance of an unhappy man.

'Well, you walked the plank easily enough, but you're

meant to "wax drowsy" in the bows, not behave as if you've been knocked unconscious,' said the Caliph.

'All right, all right,' replied Sinbad.

Other members of the cast were taking up bar space, followed by some of the stage crew. Bill Jones and Reg were the last to come in.

'Here's trouble,' hummed the Caliph.

Bill's ponytail bobbed up and down as he crossed the floor. He removed his outside coat with difficulty. 'A total disaster,' he said. 'If the critics had been in, they would have cooked us.'

Reg edged his chair closer to Bill's, peering anxiously through his glasses at whoever spoke. He gave a tut every now and then because he didn't know what else to do.

'If the critics had been in,' said the Caliph, 'they would be drunk by now, like I intend to be soon.'

'All right, all right,' Sinbad growled again.

Reg took a sip of his lager. 'I thought . . .' he said and then paused. 'I thought the show went quite well and the plot keeps people in suspense. Look at the stage effects.' There was no reaction to this.

Bill tapped Reg on the head. He wasn't being friendly. 'The kids are behaving like they're watching a pantomime, not taking part in one,' he said. 'As for that oddball, Jonathan, he was way out of line. Lost his placing completely.'

'So would you, if your hoist hadn't arrived,' replied the Caliph. 'He's got something going for him, you mark my words. Anyway, we know a dress rehearsal is always bad news.'

Sparks in the grate were catching onto a log thrown across the fire. Underneath were smaller pieces of wood, some burnt all the way through. When prodded, these would fall away to ash and smoulder long after the last customers had gone. A spark flew out of the flames and landed on the carpet at Bill's feet. He rubbed at it vigorously.

Reg took Bill's arm, as if he were a young child. He wanted to make him feel better.'We're going to have a great show,' he said. Reg stood up. 'Diddle de ho!' he sang.

'I'll have a port and lemon, please, Reg,' said the Caliph. 'And put your best foot forward.' He settled himself more comfortably, ready for the evening's entertainment.

'Have you just farted?' Sinbad asked.

The Caliph glared at his friend of many years. 'Certainly not!' he said.

Back at the Morrison household, Jonathan was in an

extreme state of depression.

His parents didn't understand how badly the show had gone and he was coming to realise a few hard facts about life.

You couldn't rely on other people. One of the stage crew had just let Jonathan down very badly indeed and there was no reason to suppose that anything would be different on the first night.

He saw a whole host of problems arising, with him and possibly Amy in the middle of them. At least Princess Pearl hadn't fallen over under his leadership. But their duet lacked any sort of togetherness and Miss Spencer hadn't been around to say goodbye on leaving the theatre. A bad sign.

Jonathan felt that his career was already over.

'Would you like some more supper, love?' asked Mrs Morrison.

How could his mother talk about such trifles now? Jonathan was fed up with watching his father and Alex play football amongst the furniture. He was the odd man out. As usual, they were just being silly.

'Steady,' said Mr Morrison.

He caught the ball and gave it a couple of bounces before tossing it back to Alex. Alex skipped sideways and, without warning, lowered himself into a roly-poly somersault.

'What's that for?' called Mr Morrison.

He kicked the ball out of Alex's grip as they rolled over the sofa and both of them were laughing.

Although Jonathan had his father and his best friend here, he might as well have been a stranger. A stranger in his own home! None of them realised that he was about to embark on the biggest ordeal of his life and that nothing would be the same again.

When the telephone rang, Mrs Morrison answered, nodding in Jonathan's direction.

'Sam's mother from New York,' she said.

Alex and Jonathan exchanged a look.

'Uh oh,' said Alex.

He had taken the ball back and was balancing it on the end of his right trainer. Mr Morrison pushed Alex gently away from the dishwasher as he took their dinner plates from the kitchen table and went to stack them.

'Hi,' said Jonathan into the receiver.

'Hi, honey!' said Sam's mother.

Jonathan had to wait a moment to hear her.

'Honey, I'm ringing to wish you all the luck in the world. Sam has told me how you've had to take over the lead and I'm just so happy for you. This is a wonderful opportunity . . .'

Jonathan paused. 'I haven't got the main part . . .'

'Well, honey, you must have the talent to get that far. Believe me, you're going places. Do you have an agent?'

'No,' said Jonathan.

'Honey, you've got to have an agent. Let me give you a few names when I next visit. Don't forget, I started out as Cinderella and I had great press.'

'OK,' said Jonathan.

'Sweetie, a big kiss from me . . . I'll be thinking of you tomorrow night.'

Jonathan put the receiver down with a click.

'What did she say?' asked Alex.

'She said I should get an agent.'

'What for?' asked Alex.

'Because agents persuade managers to hire you,' Jonathan replied. 'Mia says that they have their own private cubicles for lunch in restaurants.'

'She must have huge telephone bills,' Alex said.

Jonathan could imagine Sam's mother calling friends throughout the western hemisphere.

'I think she's really sad,' Alex said.

Mrs Morrison pushed the two boys towards the door

of the sitting room. Alex was staying the night, but both boys were reluctant to go.

'Time for bed,' she said firmly.

Jonathan took Barnaby from his box. The guinea pig was drowsy and his whiskers bristled from the effect of being moved. As the boys went upstairs, he gave Jonathan what might have been a sympathetic lick and clung to his shoulder.

'Barnaby is not sleeping on your bed,' Mrs Morrison called out from behind them.

'OK, Mum,' said Jonathan.

In his room, he opened a drawer full of his dance gear and took out a bag of yoghurt drops. He lay some on the duvet and the guinea pig gobbled them all up and then ground his teeth.

'That means he wants more,' Jonathan told Alex.

He crouched beside Barnaby, stroking his fur until he felt a bit sleepy. Jonathan poured the rest of the packet onto the bed and took three for himself. The duvet was purple, a lucky colour, and one that wouldn't show up the guinea pig's mistakes.

'What have you done to your hair?' asked Alex, who was yawning now. 'You look like a monk.'

'Shut up,' said Jonathan.

He lay down on his front with Barnaby at his left ear. Jonathan tried to relax. He did some breathing exercises while Alex went to the bathroom, but he was too tired to turn over and do them properly.

Above him, the poster of Nureyev as Count Albrecht was not at all reassuring. He was suddenly a distant acquaintance. If only Jonathan had had an opportunity of meeting him man to man, of discussing issues such as stage fright and the pettiness of fellow performers.

If only Nureyev was still alive. Jonathan would have waited for him at the stage door of the Royal Opera House and got his autograph.

Chapter Twenty-Seven

December eighteenth. Seven p.m. There were crowds outside the Albany Theatre, all arriving for the first performance of *Sinbad The Sailor.*

At the entrance, cars drove into the forecourt and then on towards underground parking. Mothers and fathers with children made their way through snow and slush that had turned to grey. Again the night was cold.

Ushers in uniform were waiting to direct them. The queue at the box office was long, but already a sign had been posted: *FIRST NIGHT TICKETS SOLD OUT.*

A harassed mother had got the date wrong and was now escorting her kids out again. The two of them screamed with rage, making obstacles for those trying to enter.

'Shush!' said the mother. She kept the kids well in front of her, creating a necessary human shield.

An old woman made her way painfully to the royal circle. At the top of the steps she turned back, as though she had forgotten what she was there for. Then she went on down through the passage and out of sight.

Visitors peered at photographs of an unknown cast. Sinbad and the Caliph took equal precedence on the billboards, with Princess Pearl set between them as leading lady. Other characters had smaller pictures, and the children's names were listed neatly at the bottom.

Information on the show promised a *Spellbinding Production* and *A Miraculous Voyage of Special Effects*. The programmes being sold by young men and women gave titles to the song and dance numbers and a short history of each star.

Mr and Mrs Morrison and Mrs Nathan met up by a pillar in the first level bar as arranged. Peter wore a suit and Charmian had on a coral dress and jacket that she had bought earlier in a second-hand shop. Mrs Nathan was more revealing in navy chiffon with a plunging neckline and high-heeled shoes.

'Can't stay,' she said to them breathlessly. She gulped at her glass of white wine and put a hand up to hide her next remark. 'So glad Jonathan has had no ill effects from the accident. Mia's fine too.' Mrs Nathan beamed. 'It's all go, backstage, and those children are skipping like kangaroos with excitement. I've never seen anything like it.' She pressed her plump hands against the folds of her dress. 'Naughty me for being here,' she whispered, 'but we're well under control.'

Mrs Morrison was sure that they were. She had been told a whole week ago by Jonathan not to chaperone on the first night. Charmian didn't mind. She would rather keep her nerves together in the auditorium, surrounded by all these people.

'I won't be able to get out again,' said Mrs Nathan, 'so if you want me to give Jonathan a message, you had better let me know now.' She stood expectantly, drumming her newly varnished fingernails onto the ridges of the nearest pillar.

'Give him our love,' Mr Morrison answered. 'He knows we're here and that's good enough.'

Peter loosened his tie. He had no idea how he was going to last the length of the show. Mr Morrison hated crowds and the thought of his son on stage was producing a conflict of emotions.

Mrs Nathan put down her empty glass. 'Well, I shall

see you after the show,' she said and went off towards the swing doors.

As Mrs Nathan approached, a man coming from the other direction bumped straight into her.

'Oh, I'm so sorry,' she said.

The man stood back, peering down at his black shoes. 'I'm sorry,' he said. 'Please go ahead.'

'Thank you so much,' said Mrs Nathan, and she waved at the Morrisons just before she went through the doors for a second time. 'Bye,' she mouthed, and was gone.

Mr Morrison gave a sigh of relief. Then he kissed his wife briefly on the lips.

'You look stunning,' he said.

Mrs Morrison laughed. 'I feel rather underdressed compared to Mrs Nathan,' she replied.

'Thank goodness for that,' said Mr Morrison.

Theatregoers were ordering drinks for the interval from barmen who worked without a break. A child whined as he was drawn down the stairs by an adult each side of him. He had lost the power of his legs.

Backstage the tannoy prickled into action. 'Ladies and gentlemen, this is your half-hour call.'

In the girls' dressing room, Mia was applying full make-up. Next to her was a box the size of a toolkit. She had already used her beige foundation base and a pink blusher that made V lines across her cheeks. Now she put a dab of eye shadow on her lids. Mia's hair was pulled back into a half ponytail with a scrunchie to hold it in place.

She pouted at the mirror. 'My mouth's too big,' she said.

The other girls didn't answer. They too were searching for colour palettes and liner pencils.

'You need more mascara,' Mia said to Amy, who was sitting opposite her.

'Much more,' said another girl. The girl was very thin and had soot-coloured eyelashes that gave her the appearance of a doll. She was stretching out in the corner.

Mrs Nathan had appeared. 'Make sure you all have your fringes pinned back,' she said. 'I've brought some extra grips.' She checked her daughter's hair and then gave her a peck on the forehead.

'Go away, Mum,' said Mia. She wiped the lipstick from her face.

Over in the boys' dressing room, Jonathan felt decidedly light-headed. Perhaps the bump in the car had got to him after all. It didn't help either having make-up on that suggested a bad case of jaundice. Jonathan wanted to pee very badly, but when he went to the loo, he couldn't go.

Zak kept whistling. The boys were dressed for the courtiers scene and comparing their harem pants.

'Anyone for Coke?' asked Cameron. His shaved head shone like a beacon. He took some drink down until he burped and then gave the bottle to Zak.

'Yo,' said Zak. He did the same and passed the Coke to Jonathan.

On stage, Bill was making sure that the Caliph's throne had an appropriate cushion in case of backache. Then he gave the thumbs up to an electrician just within his sight. Props people still went about the stage, re-focussing lamps and testing mikes.

The band had begun to play a medley of tunes, the synthesised violins being dominant.

Bill's assistant was worried. 'Reg is not in the pit,' she said. 'He's not in his room either.'

'Well, find him,' said Bill. 'We're on any moment.'

The assistant ran off stage. Bill could hear her calling for him and swore under his breath. He had never known Reg to be so unreliable.

Somebody near the front of house had a cough, a terrible sound that reverberated through him and probably every person in the theatre. Just their luck to have someone in with bronchitis, he thought.

Reg had wandered onto the stage at last. 'I'm here,' he said. He was shuffling about. Reg wore a dinner jacket and a bow tie. His gaze was vacant through his spectacles.

'Pull yourself together,' Bill growled in desperation.

'I'm trying,' replied Reg. 'Are you all right?'

'Of course I'm not all right,' Bill said. He had a sudden desire to hit Reg.

'I'm off, then,' Reg went on, rather uncertainly.

'It's *Sinbad The Sailor*, remember?' Bill called after him but Reg had already gone.

'Ladies and gentlemen, this is your five-minute call,' announced the tannoy.

There was no more time.

Jonathan and the boys had met with other members of the cast as they filed past. In tandem they came up the stairs, jostling for space and chattering.

Miss Spencer waited for them at the top. Briefly Jonathan caught her eye and he was sad for reasons that he could not understand. She wore a diamond pendant at her throat that shone in the darkness.

'Absolute silence from now on,' she said and then

whispered 'Good luck.' Her gaze held Jonathan's again. He felt sure of it.

Then he was swept on as though by a tide, until quite by accident he found himself in the left wing with Zak and Cameron. They clutched hands briefly.

A last call from the tannoy. 'Ladies and gentlemen, overture and beginners, please, for Act One.' The Caliph took to his throne, majestic in full regalia. The Wazir stood next to him, and Princess Pearl, with a veil for camouflage, appeared to be making a last adjustment to her bodice.

Jonathan felt someone pinching his bottom. Amy was beside him.

'Good luck,' she said.

He tried to answer her but his mouth had frozen and the curtain was rising to a gasp of pleasure from the audience.

The Wazir came forward with his arms outstretched.

The show was on.

Chapter Twenty-Eight

The Wazir spoke. 'The Peacock of the Silver Path, the Lion of the Golden Throne, the Ruler of the World, the Descendant of the Prophet, Haroun al Rashid, Ibn Abdullah, Ibn Abbas, Ibn Majomet – the Caliph!' The Wazir was bowing with a flourish.

The Caliph got off his throne to give a curt nod in response. 'Bring me to my harem that I may transport myself in heavenly delights!'

The girls were ahead with veils flowing and, from their midst, Princess Pearl had risen to perform a snaky number in front of her father. But she was disguised and he didn't recognise her.

'Let that beauty come to my quarters at ten-thirty

tonight,' he commanded the Wazir. The Caliph clapped his hands and the girls took positions of repose. The Wazir was not happy. He knew the true identity of the saucy Princess Pearl.

Jonathan came out of the wings with Zak and Cameron to sit at the foot of the Caliph's throne. He had made it! He was on stage and his first impression was one of dazzling brightness. The lights blinded him. Jonathan didn't dare move. He had no idea what would happen next but his reaction was to sit very still.

Thankfully, the Caliph was in charge. His courtiers were deferential to the point of fear. He sauntered about as if the décor of plush satin curtain and the gilt settee were his personal possessions.

As the musical tempo changed, so came the moment when Jonathan must move. He and the other courtiers were being drawn into line by the Wazir.

Yes, Jonathan could remember what to do . . . but the lights were too strong . . .

Step, brush, step, he went with the others. They were downstage before they knew it. Step, brush, step . . . Now the courtiers faced the audience with only the pit between them.

Jonathan heard the coughing and his heart sank. In

that second, the Caliph's Court was replaced by evidence of his day-to-day living. Jonathan could recognise that cough anywhere. He caught sight of Jason's cap twitching in the front row. Hugs Bug was probably right behind him and choking to death. Well, Jonathan hoped her demise would be quick. In no time there would be a parade of white handkerchiefs.

He must concentrate . . .

Step, brush, step, rise . . . hold . . . step, brush, step, step.

There was a certain rhythm to this that he liked . . .

Jonathan found himself off stage again. Had his quick entrance and exit been a dream?

'It's great,' he said but nobody seemed to be listening.

Miss Spencer was there for them. 'Hurry for your next change,' she said.

The audience were laughing. A rise and fall of noise that sent shivers down Jonathan's spine. He didn't dare look at the first row in case he recognised more schoolmates, but he knew they were there. Just once he heard yelps that were a definite sign of Sam's appreciation.

Princess Pearl spoke rudely to the Caliph, but he was implacable. He would not let his daughter leave the court in case she misbehaved. He had prospective suitors for her to see. Soon Sinbad would arrive and invite the Royal Family to his ship. So far, Jonathan thought, so good.

When he came off stage again, Mrs Nathan was there to tackle him on his way down. She was a large apparition in chiffon.

'Don't forget to smile,' she urged Jonathan, as if she were speaking from the experience of elocution.

'I am,' he replied.

'Out of the way, please,' said a technician. He was trying to pass Mrs Nathan with a palm tree.

'So sorry,' muttered Mrs Nathan. 'Move now, children.'

The kids took no notice. They were watching Sinbad and Prince Hassan. This was their naughty joke routine. But the jokes weren't new and, at one point, the audience groaned.

'They're meant to laugh,' said Mia and her eyes were saucers in the dark.

Reg's piano music was coming through loud and clear. He would be very hyped up for the storm about to break.

The scene change came so quickly that there was a gasp as the throne room cloth flew out and the boat came into view. Hefty waves spread across the canvas at the back. Sinbad walked the plank to show his men what would happen to them if they disobeyed and then he made it back again.

'Phew,' said Cameron, who stood next to Jonathan, ready for the hornpipe.

Jonathan wondered what his father would make of the boat that was about to sail. He couldn't fail to be interested in having his own son on deck. Jonathan still felt strange but his nerves had given way to excitement.

Prince Hassan was already asking for the hand of the Caliph's daughter.

The Caliph thought for a long time. 'As ruler of the principality, I order you to sail fast overseas. Seek the treasure that is mine, and my daughter you will win in time.' Up and down the deck went the Caliph. He had a lot of stamina.

Some little boy called out from the audience. 'Is the boat going to sink?'

The Caliph gave him an appreciative nod. 'Not with me on board!' he shouted.

The audience cheered. He was a naughty man and they were loving him.

Only if Prince Hassan found the diamond Moor-El-Din, hidden in a far distant valley, would he be allowed to marry Princess Pearl.

The voyage was about to begin.

Miss Spencer beckoned to Jonathan as he came off stage after the hornpipe. He didn't want to talk to her because his mind was on his next change. Jonathan tried to smile.

'Good luck,' she said. 'You can do it.'

Nothing more. No direction or advice on his solo, just a confidence in him, which made Jonathan want to hug her. Miss Spencer at that moment was an angel in the wings.

He was late. The other kids were waiting as he joined them in his shorts and T-shirt. The storm had begun.

A crash of thunder made everybody jump and the entire crew were running helter-skelter. Cymbals coincided with lightning flashes and as the drums rolled, a pair of talons appeared with a blood-curdling scream. It was the Roc bird, and after that, the blackout came suddenly.

'Come on,' called Mia.

She was ahead in her gossamer robe. Other sea nymphs followed soundlessly and when the lights came up again, their surroundings were the bottom of the sea.

'I want soft winds over the Atlantic,' said the Peri sweetly. She moved forward to wave the length of the auditorium.

Jonathan could only be casual and ignore her. His fight was coming up with the Old Man of the Sea, who had brought about the bad weather. He stepped out. The spotlight fell directly on him and his enemy. The Old Man's face was contorted with rage. They were circling one another like two dogs and Jonathan felt as though the audience was on his side. A surge of power took over, as though his body were being manipulated without his control.

Jonathan ran from where he was, increasing his speed until without knowing it, he was into a series of leaps and moving weightlessly through the crescendo of the music. Each time Jonathan touched the surface of the stage, he spun around once to take off again. The leaps split wider apart until his legs burnt with the effort.

The Old Man was in his path. Jonathan picked up his sword from behind a rock and they came very close together. The Old Man also had a weapon. They were fencing now warily and there were shouts from the stalls. Jonathan was sure he could hear Sam shouting over the others, 'Kill him! Kill him!'

When he lunged at his opponent, the Old Man fell back, first in horror and then with a stupefied expression, as though he could not help himself. Afterwards, he lay very still. The sea nymphs surrounded his body, making a bower.

And then it happened.

As Jonathan withdrew his sword in triumph, the blade snapped in half. Lifting it high, the disaster was made worse. Jonathan was slipping too.

He didn't wait for the reaction. Jonathan took a quick bow and ran off the stage. If anybody had clapped, he couldn't hear a sound. His whole fight had been a charade.

Mrs Nathan was in the way again. 'Never mind, dear,' she said. 'You couldn't help it.' Her bosoms heaved sympathetically through the chiffon.

Jonathan strode past her and left his weapon on the spot as he did so. He couldn't speak. The horror of his mishap was with him all the way to the dressing room.

'My sword broke,' Jonathan said to the Parkview boys.

'Forget it,' advised Cameron. 'Worse things can happen.

Zak was pulling on flesh-coloured tights. He gave a small whistle. They didn't care, either of them.

The interval was announced. Once again, Jonathan saw himself in the mirror at the wrong time. His hair flopped just short of his ears. How could he be a ballet dancer when so many things went wrong that weren't even his fault?

Jonathan couldn't blame his father for being rude about the profession. He was right. Doing ballet made him look ridiculous. Imagine if he had been dancing Spartacus!

He'd made up his mind. Jonathan would tell Dad that he had made a mistake and that he wasn't going to be a dancer after all.

But there was still the second half.

Jonathan hesitated as he closed the door behind him. With any luck he might wake up from one of his worst nightmares.

'Hello, hello, hello!' The Caliph had stopped in front of him in the passage, resplendent in full costume. Jonathan noticed first the shiny pasted jewels that cut across his turban.

'I hear the leaps are going very well.' His was a statement, not a question. The Caliph's eyebrows had risen to charcoal points on his forehead.

'No, they're not,' said Jonathan. 'My sword broke and everybody laughed and I don't want to go back on stage. I feel sick.' Jonathan couldn't remember much about his solo beforehand. Nothing mattered now. 'All my form is out there!' he went on.

'Ah,' said the Caliph. 'Did you hear people laughing?'

'No,' replied Jonathan. 'But they must have done.'

For a big man, the Caliph moved surprisingly fast. He swung his dressing-room door open and beckoned Jonathan inside. 'What you need is a dose of my magic mixture,' he said. The Caliph poured some thick, white substance into a glass.

Then he added water and gave the concoction a stir. 'This will do the trick,' he said, handing the glass to Jonathan.

Perhaps the Caliph was a magician in another disguise. 'Is this a drug?' Jonathan asked.

'No drugs, but there's a touch of Milk of Magnesia as well as one or two other ingredients of mine. Works wonders for the stomach.'

Jonathan emptied the chalky mixture into his mouth. If he waited here long enough, he might miss the rest of the performance.

'Now,' said the Caliph, 'are you coming with me? We've got work to do.'

The Caliph took Jonathan by the shoulder and together they went back up the stairs.

The second half of the pantomime was minutes away. Members of the cast were going to their positions and somewhere in that twilight world backstage, Jonathan was aware of the sound of rolling machinery.

He wondered what would happen next. Jonathan had an idea. If he didn't make it as a ballet dancer, maybe one day he could play the Caliph.

Chapter Twenty-Nine

As the curtain went up, the Peri's wish for fair weather had been answered. The stage was lit with soft peach shades suggesting a warmer climate and the tropics. The boards were bare. No props. A silence that could be heard.

Everybody had gathered. In the wings, there was a sense of impending excitement at the critical scene about to take place.

Jonathan could see the glint of Bill's white shirt under his dinner jacket and Miss Spencer on the opposite site, sparkling diamonds.

It was funny how the details struck him. Amy clutching her long trader's skirt . . . Evangeline's nose just in sight behind the crowd . . . The smell of wood and machinery in their standing area.

Bill had given his sign for Jonathan to begin.

But still the boy didn't move. He was frozen. Even the flutter of Princess Pearl's tutu was unfamiliar, a preparation that had nothing to do with him.

'Off you go!' The Caliph was prodding him in the back.

'Get a life!' hissed another voice.

Mia . . . always Mia there to irritate him. She was in the wrong place and mocking Jonathan . . . a merchant's trollop with bad intentions ready for the market scene.

He moved out from the rest of them.

Just Jonathan on his own.

Mr and Mrs Morrison watched their son from the first row of the dress circle. Peter was not a man to pray, but tonight the plea for help came instinctively. Nor did he know exactly what he was praying for. Peter heard the sharp intake of breath from Charmian next to him. They were in this together.

The short, stocky figure was almost centre stage. Any initial hesitation had disappeared. Jonathan was gathering pace as though to make up for the introduction.

His circle was very wide. Princess Pearl was coming

to meet him with feet that hardly touched the ground. Jonathan drew away as she zig-zagged about him. He was her rescuer and yet she was afraid. Her *pirouette* landed close enough to create a breeze from her spinning.

Jonathan took Princess Pearl's hand and they ran, and the music went with them. The flute brought a plaintive air that gave an inkling of more trials to come. Such freedom would never last.

Holding Princess Pearl round the waist, Jonathan felt bolder. This was no make believe. His contact with the Princess was real business and a matter of life or death. He mustn't let go.

Right now, he knew exactly how Nureyev would have dealt with his own partners. As the strong man he was prepared for every eventuality. The audience were clapping them. There was no mistake. Jonathan wanted the *pas de deux* to go on. But he was to make way for Prince Hassan and now they were a metre apart.

Jonathan came off stage as the Prince came on.

The skies were darkening.

The lovers met and more blood-curdling screams announced the Roc's arrival. His talons were ready to pounce on the unsuspecting Princess.

The blackout took place as Jonathan was being fitted into his harness.

'Ooooooh,' sighed the audience.

'Ready, son?' asked the technician, who had made sure he was safe for travel.

Jonathan's reply was lost.

Now the hoist was taking him without further delay, and in those seconds of entering the light again, he thought he had gone blind.

The further up he went, the brighter they were. The heat was intense. A fanfare of cries accompanied him and as he climbed, Jonathan's view was different from that of the rehearsal. This was a new world and the chance to take in hundreds of people. Tonight he was airborne and famous as the boy in space.

Jonathan's legs moved separately from the rest of him, weightless again and swinging, though he tried to keep them together as Miss Spencer had told him.

He stared out into the auditorium and saw only a vast arena of forms without faces. Jonathan tried to make out his friends in the first row but they too were dark.

Was his father with him now? Did he understand that Jonathan had no alternative but to be here?

He was halfway across.

After this passage, he would join Sinbad and Hassan for the traders' gathering before they set off on their final haul to the Valley of Diamonds. Unbeknown to them, Princess Pearl was travelling not far behind. She was soon to be reunited with her prince.

As the full width of the stage stretched below him, Jonathan had the feeling that he could stay here for ever. The strobes were creating fantastic patterns marking his entry into a new world.

Far below him, a smile played on Miss Spencer's lips. Her illness was never far away, but for now she had forgotten it. Jonathan's future was clear to her. After his solo and the duet, there was no question.

'Well?' she said.

Bill Jones was watching Jonathan too. 'Yes,' he murmured. 'I was wrong. He's good. Very good.'

The mortal world was vanishing before Jonathan. A strange apparition had crossed his gaze. A woman whose physical structure couldn't be determined and yet he felt he had known her all his life. The figure was Michelle Kavinska, his grandmother. She was there like a ghost, all in white and gracefully flowing alongside him. Her eyes were those of his father's . . . brown and soulful. The similarity was obvious.

There was no mistaking her presence. Jonathan felt a bond beyond his understanding that gave him the promise of love.

Mr Morrison glimpsed her too from where he sat, the figure absent from him for so many years. There she was, floating . . . and if he reached out . . . he might catch her still.

'She's there, look!' he said pointing. His throat was dry.

'Who?' asked Mrs Morrison. 'I can't see anyone.' She couldn't understand him.

A distant drumbeat came from the band in the pit. The audience had begun to clap as they waited for Jonathan.

He was descending and aware of coming home.

Michelle Kavinska waved to him from a great height, now a cloudy figure. She was on her way.

Jonathan waved back and looking for the last time, he saw only the space and the stars where he had been.

Acknowledgements

My thanks are due to the following people for their encouragement and support: Andrea Rayner, who edited the original manuscript; 'Foxy' and Peter Alexander; Alexander Koby for photography. And to the late Jack and Mollie Penycate for allowing me to quote from their work.

About the Author

CELIA PURCELL trained in ballet, turning later to Contemporary Dance, where she performed in venues ranging from theatres to open fields. She has taught widely – in London, Tehran and Calgary, Canada. She is a published poet and now runs a Contemporary Art Gallery. This is her first novel. Celia lives in London.